D1187349

BBC

DOCTOR WHO

The Legends of Ashildr

BBC

DOCTOR WHO

The Legends of Ashildr

1 3 5 7 9 10 8 6 4 2

BBC Books, an imprint of Ebury Publishing
20 Vauxhall Bridge Road,
London SW1V 2SA

BBC Books is part of the Penguin Random House group of companies whose addresses can be found at global.penguinrandomhouse.com

Doctor Who is a BBC Wales production
Executive producers: Steven Moffat and Brian Minchin

First published by BBC Books in 2015

www.eburypublishing.co.uk

A CIP catalogue record for this book is available from the British Library

ISBN 9781785940576

Editorial director: Albert DePetrillo
Series consultant: Justin Richards
Project editor: Steve Tribe
Cover design: Lee Binding © Woodland Books Ltd, 2015
Production: Alex Goddard

Typeset in India by Thomson Digital Pvt Ltd, Noida, Delhi

Printed and bound in the U S A

CONTENTS

INTRODUCTION

She is known by many names – the girl who died, the woman who lived – but the earliest, her *real* name, seems to have been Ashildr. There are stories and legends, myths and tales dating back from the present day to Viking times. Far too many tales to recount in a single volume like this one.

So instead we have brought together just four stories, four legends of Ashildr. They come from different times in her tremendously long life, though all from the earlier part of it. They are reproduced from different sources.

The first two stories – 'The Arabian Knightmare' and 'The Fortunate Isles' – have come to us through third parties. As a result, we cannot vouch for their authenticity or guarantee that everything, or indeed anything, in these stories actually happened.

The final two stories – 'The Triple Knife' and 'The Ghosts of Branscombe Wood' – are taken directly from Ashildr's own journals. Again, even though the incidents they describe are recounted by Ashildr herself, we cannot be completely certain that what she wrote in her journals was the actual truth.

But whether they are all true, partly fabricated, or complete fiction, these are four of the tales that have contributed to the renowned Legends of Ashildr.

The Arabian Knightmare

James Goss

Once long ago and very far away there was a King. For there are always kings. This King of Samarkand ruled from the sands of Persia to the walls of China, from the plains of Araby to the shores of the Ganges herself. He ruled places with poetic names, because he loved to be entertained.

This King had a problem – he ruled the most romantic places in the world, and yet he was bored. So bored was he that he offered his hand in marriage to the woman who could keep him amused. And, sad to say, no woman could. Every day his Vizier brought him a new wife, and every evening, the King shook his head and cut off his wife's. The much-widowed King became even more bored, and the Vizier became worried – for the King had started looking interestedly at the Vizier's daughters.

One day the King was walking through the market place when he espied a pair of beautiful eyes watching him from a window. As no one ever met his eyes, the King was startled, and ceased his walk.

'Who are you that looks at me so?' he demanded.

A woman's voice laughed down at him. 'I have an answer to your question, oh King of Samarkand. You wonder why every woman bores you, do you not?'

'I do,' sighed the King. 'It is a vexing problem.'

'It is because all your brides are too frightened to speak.' The face in shadow laughed. 'But I am not afraid of you. If you will call me down, then I shall never bore you.'

The King looked at the figure. All he could see of this woman were her eyes. They were, he thought, very pretty eyes. The King of Samarkand laughed. 'Very well. Come down and be my Queen.'

And so the woman did, and she was very beautiful. The King marvelled at the wisdom of his choice. Her eyes were the softest silver, her complexion clear, her smile intelligent.

'I am the Lady Sherade,' she announced. 'Come let us go to your palace and be married and I shall tell you tales of marvels with which to enchant the night...'

And so she began...

The Last Voyage of Sindbad

'You have heard of the voyages of Sindbad the Sailor...?' And so began the first tale of the Lady Sherade.

In the times of the Caliph Haroun al-Raschid there lived in Baghdad the mightiest sailor, adventurer and merchant the world has ever known. His name was Sindbad, and he had voyaged far and wide over every sea upon which the sun shone.

One day there came to his doorway a young servant called Dash. The servant was drawn in by the scent of rosewater steaming up from the hot flagstones. On spying Dash, a handsome man came to the door.

'Who are you that lingers at this doorway? Do you not know that it is the doorway of Sindbad the Sailor who has voyaged far and wide over every sea?'

Young Dash did indeed know this and said so, and furthermore added, 'And, my lord, I know that you yourself are no less than Sindbad himself.'

At that Sindbad laughed, for he had a good sense of humour. 'My servants are asleep, for I was entertaining them into the night with tales of my voyages and so I must break my own fast. Will you join me for some food, stranger?'

Dash gladly assented and the two sat down in a courtyard that smelt richly of aloe wood and flowers. Sindbad brought out a meal that was both lavish and delightful and the sailor told him many stories about himself and his wonderful voyages. When they had both eaten their full, he pushed back his plate and surveyed the stranger. 'So, young man – how came you to my doors? Do you seek service?'

Dash laughed. 'Well, I'd better, since you have no other servants.'

Sindbad bowed. 'You have uncovered my untruth. But why should I when I can cook so well?'

'You have no servants, my lord and also no wife?'

Here Sindbad stopped smiling. 'I have had many servants and also many wives. Sadly, whenever I head out on a voyage, all my servants are eaten by cannibals or carried away by giant birds, and when I finally make my way home, my wives have either died or thought me dead and remarried.' He sighed. 'Ah well. So much for them. I must make my own way in the world.'

'I see.' Dash nodded. 'And are you quite done with adventure?'

'Why do you ask?' said Sindbad with keen interest. 'Is it simple chance, or has God himself brought you here?'

'You are as clever as the market traders claim,' the young servant smiled. 'I have heard, oh master, of a distant land where rests a marvellous wealth of treasure. I would undertake the voyage there.'

'And so you came to me?' Sindbad asked.

'Indeed, oh lord.'

'Or did you petition every other boatman before coming to me?'

The young servant made no answer.

And so Sindbad the Sailor and Dash the servant set out on a great voyage. It went much as Sindbad's voyages normally did. Within a few days the ship was caught up in a storm, and only by the hand of providence did a few survivors make it to shore, where they were picked off by vast and hungry serpents.

'I knew I should never have come with you,' wailed the navigator as he vanished into the serpent's maw, leaving Sindbad and Dash alone.

They clambered up a tree out of the reach of the serpents, and, while the servant got his breath back, Sindbad lamented his fate. 'Why does this always happen to me?'

'You are,' Dash agreed as the serpents snapped at their heels, 'somewhat unlucky.'

Sindbad surveyed Dash curiously. 'I wonder how much of this is your doing,' he remarked. 'After all, you are no servant boy.'

'Oh, so you'd noticed,' Dash nodded.

'I'm not blind, girl.' Sindbad laughed, poking a snake with a branch. 'You need have no fear of me marrying you. Tell me, who are you?'

'My name is Ash El Dir,' the servant said. 'And much, my lord, of what I have told you is true. I have travelled far and wide. My last master was a man called Ali-Baba. I did him much service. He and I discovered the fabled hoard of the Ancient Guild of Thieves, kept in a cave which only opened magically to a voice. I urged Ali-Baba to caution in what he took away, but he scooped up armfuls, and, when the thieves discovered the theft, they were able to follow the tracks of our laden mules. Ali-Baba and his wife had fallen asleep after celebrating their good fortune, and it was left to me to tidy up after their party. It was then that I noticed how full the courtyard was, because a travelling merchant had begged leave to store forty barrels of oil there overnight. As I went around tidying, I noticed that one of the barrels moved slightly, and I began to suspect the awful truth – that the Ancient Guild of Thieves had found us and were waiting to murder us in our sleep. So, I figured, as the barrels were supposed to contain oil, perhaps they should.'

'You drowned them in oil?' Sindbad ceased looking at the snakes and instead stared at Ash in alarm.

'Oh no, that would be a waste of good oil. So I used tar instead.'

'I see.'

'The next morning, Ali-Baba marvelled that the merchant had not returned for his barrels, and delighted to think that, in addition to his marvellous treasure, he now had forty barrels of oil. He was disappointed to find instead the barrels contained forty thieves. His wife, a rather sharper woman than he, immediately suspected my involvement and ordered me to leave. I took with me a map I had found in the Thieves' cave, which is all I had wanted.'

'So,' Sindbad wailed to God of his misfortune, 'you are using me as you have used Ali-Baba.'

'Well, yes, if you must. But, like Ali-Baba, you too will end up rich.'

'If I do not end up eaten by snakes.' Sindbad glanced down nervously. 'Tell me, girl, do you have any tar on you?'

'Oh no.' And she laughed a laugh that was like funeral music. 'I do not need it. Did you not know the fruit of this tree is poisonous? Come, let us gather it, and then we can feed the snakes…'

After many more such perilous encounters, Ash El Dir and Sindbad made their way out of the forest into a clearing. In the middle of the clearing was a pool of water clear as crystal. Sindbad, who had long suffered a terrible thirst, bent over it to drink, but Ash held him back.

'This island is strange,' she told him. 'The animals in it are large and deadly. We should be cautious.'

Sindbad laughed at the girl. 'On my voyages the animals are always large and deadly. Why, there was a time when I was captured by elephants—'

'Have you ever wondered why they're like that, though?' Ash said, continuing to hold him back. 'If it's something in the ground, seeping into what they eat and drink, then maybe we should be more careful.'

But Sindbad threw himself on the ground, drinking heavily from the crystal pool. He assured her it was the finest water he had ever tasted and mocked her caution.

'My caution?' Ash replied. 'It is my first shipwreck. By the way, look up.'

Hanging between the trees were thick strands of web.

'Imagine the spiders that could weave such a web,' laughed Sindbad.

'I am and I think we should run.'

With a rushing and chittering, the spiders came for them – and what spiders. Fierce of fang and sharp of limb, the creatures were the size of horses, but in the place of their bodies were the screaming heads of men, calling on God to have mercy on them.

'What can they be?' cried Sindbad full of woe.

'At a guess, other shipwrecked sailors,' Ash said. She dragged him into the forest, clubbing away the first of the spiders that pursued them. It had the face of a crying boy.

'I thank you,' it cried. 'I thank you for killing me.'

'To hear is to obey,' said Ash, and made an end of it.

'The poor child,' said Sindbad, beginning a lament, but Ash stopped him.

'We need to run. Also, we need more of that poison fruit.'

'You would tempt the spiders to poison apples?'

'No.' Ash pulled him on. 'The fruit's for you. You really shouldn't have swallowed that water.'

Sindbad suffered agonies of purgation long and hard, calling on God in the extremes of his torments. When he awoke from them, he was in a cave, and Ash was feeding him the last of the food from her backpack. 'Where are we?' asked Sindbad.

'A cave at the edge of the forest. The spiders don't seem to like it.'

'How did you know?'

Ash shrugged. 'I left you here. They hadn't eaten you when I came back.'

'I see.' Sindbad looked warily at the servant. 'And where did you go?'

And Ash sat down in the sand in front of Sindbad and told him thus…

The Story of the Stone Men

Beyond the woods, began Ash El Dir, was a clearing as though there had been a great fire. This was marked on my map as a perfect circle, and indeed it seemed so, although it went on for so far, the ground blackened and burnt as old cinders. I walked around the edge until I came to the figure of a Dervish, carved from stone.

'Who are you that approaches this site?' the Dervish asked me. 'It is full of danger and I would advise you to keep away.'

I produced my map and explained to the stone Dervish that I needed to go to the centre of the clearing in order to find the amethyst I sought.

'Beyond here is a crater,' the Dervish said. 'The treasure you seek lies hidden at the bottom, but, alas, young lady, I must warn you that the path is full of danger. I was placed here to guard this land. Many have attempted your quest before, and all have perished. If you will go on, you must listen to your voice and not that of those who have gone before.'

I thanked the Dervish for his words and trod on, the ground still warm beneath my feet. The crater only appeared as I came upon the very edge of it, and I made my way gently down its slopes, the pumice crumbling under foot. Shapes were planted here and there as I climbed down, and it was only when I rested my weight on one of them that I realised it was the statue of a man, but such a strange statue, made out of the same burnt ground.

The statue spoke to me. 'Heed me, voyager, for I once sought the quest as you did. I beg you to turn back, to go back, to go away. You are lost if you press on further.'

I thanked the stone man, but climbed down further.

I came to a second statue, which again exhorted me to turn back in piteous tones.

I thanked the second statue, and carried on.

I passed a third statue and then a fourth, all urging me that it was not too late to escape.

You may wonder why I did not turn back, and indeed, I thought about it. But I considered it thus – these brave adventurers had all perished in the art of turning back. Clearly, if I too gave up and turned back, I would also perish. There was something in this land, something dreadful – some dark poison which altered the animals, had turned the shipwrecked sailors into spiders, and seemingly was able to transfix men into statues. I had, perhaps, been lucky to survive this far. So I went on, figuring no harm could come to me.

I came at last to the bottom of the crater. The heat here was still extreme, and all around me were slivers of metal which would have made fine swords. At the very darkest centre of the crater were bones made of silver. The bones seemed to move and stir as I passed them, trying to draw themselves together. They grouped themselves against me, trying to stop me from crossing further – I picked up a stave of iron, and used it to ward them off, crossing past to where a dazzling orange light came. It was an amethyst, lying in the ground.

As I picked it up, the metal bones drew themselves up, for a moment forming into a great metal man, reaching out in obeisance towards me. Then they fell to the ground and were still.

Holding the amethyst, I walked back up to the top of the crater. As I passed each of the black statues, they all ceased to call out and fell silent.

At the top of the crater, the Dervish was waiting for me. 'You have not listened to me, and yet you have achieved your goal. The jewel you hold will protect you from the curse that has fallen over the island, just as it stopped you from being turned to stone.'

'I see,' I told the Dervish.

'I have one further thing to tell you,' said the Dervish. 'Others will come looking for the jewel you hold. If they ask me, I shall tell them it is gone and that you have it.'

'And I shall then, in that case, be waiting for them.'

And that is the story of how I found the amethyst which I hold here.

The Last Story of Sindbad Continues

So Ash ended her story, and Sindbad regarded her with awe and wonder, and pressed her to give him the amethyst – just to hold, but an idea seized him that he would like to possess it for ever.

'Alas my lord,' she told him. 'I fear it would do you no good. I think only I am safe to hold the stone – you are still too weak, in any case, from the curse that poisons this land.'

Sindbad agreed, and nodded, and decided to bide his time.

When he was strong enough they made their way to the shore to await rescue.

Sindbad became excited – on the horizon he could see a great iron galleon sailing towards them at great speed. He saw and he marvelled. 'We are rescued, and we may return home to Baghdad,' he cried, waving at the galleon.

But Ash held his arm and shook her head. 'That galleon sails too quickly for a normal ship,' she told him. 'Remember the warning of the Dervish – I do not trust that ship. I fear its captain knows already that I have the amethyst fashioned into an amulet and he seeks to take it from me.'

'But what can we do?'

Ash took him then to the other side of the island, and there they cut down wood. She held up the amulet and entreated with the spiders. As they had once been sailors, and because they feared the amethyst, they rushed to help her, weaving together the tree trunks into a raft with their webs, and fashioning a sail.

'If we launch from this side of the island,' said Ash, 'we may be able to escape before that iron galleon knows we have left.'

And so they set out for their voyage home.

As they rode off onto the choppy and uncertain waters, a voice echoed over the seas to them. It cried in tones of utter blackness: 'I am the Wizard of Marabia, the last true ruler of the Nile and I must have the amulet. Bring it to me.'

Storms took them away from the voice, and on into greater dangers.

And so ended the last voyage of Sindbad, as told by the Lady Sherade.

The Vizier and the Magician

Delighted by what he had heard, the Mighty King let Sherade live to tell another story. 'My lord,' she began, 'Sindbad and his servant Ash escaped from the mysterious Iron Galleon of the Mighty Wizard of Marabia...'

Their boat of twigs and spider's web brought them through a storm, but after that they feared greatly for their lives, and Sindbad fell into great lamentations as the web started to snap and the boat began to sink. Just when he feared all was lost, a passing merchant ship came onto the horizon and rescued them.

The master of the vessel offered them easy hospitality and to bring them back to Baghdad. 'My honoured guests,' he ventured, 'would you care to inspect the cargo? For there are some barrels I found floating in the sea that puzzle me.'

Sindbad saw and was delighted. 'Why,' he exclaimed, 'this is the cargo from my wrecked ship. I am not ruined after all!' He was quickly able to identify the cargo, and all aboard declared him a lucky man. Especially the servant Ash El Dir.

'That's unusual,' she said, eyeing her lord suspiciously.

Sindbad seemed untroubled. 'It is always happening to me,' he informed her. 'It is the kind of luck I have.'

Sindbad's miraculous return to Baghdad was greeted with joy and surprise by the merchants of the port, but the famous sailor hurried home to his garden which smelt of aloes and sandalwood. 'I am done with voyaging,' he declared. 'I shall cook us a feast.'

'No, let me, my lord,' insisted Ash. 'You are still weak from your sufferings on the cursed island.'

'And yet,' Sindbad tossed a handful of cargo into the air, 'I am feeling much better.'

'Perhaps it is the amulet,' Ash ventured. 'It is regrowing your vitals, like a sapling in a new season.'

'Oh, how lucky!' cried Sindbad. 'This amulet shall keep me alive all the days that are sent by God. The Destroyer of Delights shall never visit my door.'

Ash chuckled at his good humour. 'I pray not, my lord,' she told him. 'For ever is not to be lived but endured. It is not for simple men.'

'Nor servant girls either,' laughed Sindbad, his eyes quick to follow the amulet around her neck.

No sooner had Ash brought out many fine dishes for the sailor to enjoy than there was a knock at the door. 'It is late,' said Ash. 'Are you expecting anyone, my lord?' She called through the door: 'In the name of my master, who is there?'

'We are but three simple travelling merchants who seek to touch the hem of Sindbad the Sailor, whom we have heard has lately returned safe.'

'Oh Lord of Damnations,' lamented Sindbad. 'It is the Caliph.'

'How so?'

'Everyone knows that the Caliph Haroun al-Raschid, his Vizier Jafar and his Executioner go out at night in disguise,' hissed Sindbad. 'They will keep us up all night eating all this food – go, let them in, and don't, oh don't let on that you know their disguise.'

Ash unbolted the door and made formal greetings to the three merchants, offering them hospitality and refreshment.

'Why thank you,' nodded the Caliph. 'It is most kind of you. We are simple humble travelling merchants and we seek but a glass to wash the dust from our throats and a morsel of bread. I say, are those honeyed fowl?' And with that, he and his companions fell to, and Ash was kept busy running back and forth from the kitchens producing every kind of sweetmeat and sherbet that the Caliph could imagine.

Eventually he patted his stomach and professed himself delighted. 'Now, my dear, dear Sindbad. Even such humble travelling merchants as myself have heard of the stories of your voyage. Is it true you have endured another? We must be the first to hear it!'

And so Sindbad related the story of his last voyage. Ash stood by, filling the glasses, and noticing that, perhaps, her role in matters was somewhat reduced in the telling. Sindbad finished by explaining to the Caliph how he had put out the eyes of the giant spiders, escaped from the stone soldiers, and outsailed the mighty ship of iron.

'All to bring home an amulet?' The Caliph sighed with delight. 'Why such a jewel is a rich gift indeed. May I see it?'

At Sindbad's command, Ash brought forward the amethyst, and the Caliph marvelled at it.

'Truly, it is a unique stone, is it not?' he said, passing it to his Vizier and the Royal Executioner.

Both agreed that it was.

The Caliph rocked back on his heels considering. 'Funnily enough, I have heard that the Caliph's son, the handsome Prince Karim, is about to celebrate his birthday, and his father has searched high and low for a gift that would please him. I'm sure he would see it as a great favour if you were to suddenly decide to have your slave girl take it to Prince Karim.'

Ash stared at the Caliph with full alarm, and Sindbad made a face of dolorous misery.

'This is no ordinary amulet…' began Sindbad.

'I can see that. Stand closer, so that you may view its marvels,' clapped the Caliph, motioning for the Executioner to stand behind Sindbad.

Sindbad hastily instructed the girl to take the amethyst to the palace.

'We'll look after your master until you come back,' commanded the Caliph. He nodded again to the Executioner, who moved even closer to Sindbad. 'When you come back, you will find that no harm has come to him.'

So, sick of heart and furious of face, Ash took her leave of the Caliph and headed to the Palace…

'This is all very well!' laughed the Mighty King as Sherade paused in her tale. 'But what of the Wizard of Marabia?'

'I was coming to that,' said the Lady.

'And also, what of Prince Karim and the cunning servant girl, Ash El Dir? Are you to tell me of love? For there must always be love. I command you to tell me of the true love between man and woman or die.'

'To hear is to obey, my husband,' said the Lady Sherade.

The Path of Love

'So, sick of heart and furious of face, Ash El Dir took her leave of the Caliph and headed to the Palace...' continued the Lady Sherade.

Her heart beat furiously. She finally had the amethyst that she sought, the strange amulet glowing brightly in her pocket. She could escape, she could simply run away and leave Sindbad to his fate. So much for him. And yet there was within her that which liked to win.

Entrance to the palace was easy, for the Caliph had sent word ahead that she was coming with a gift for his son. Soon she found herself in the magnificent tower where the Prince spent his days in drinking and feasting, when he was not out hunting drugged animals or attacking straw dummies with scimitars.

Prince Karim stood on a balcony with his back to her, playing a musical lament of such beauty that Ash paused and stood in amazement. He sang in a beautiful voice that was heartbreaking to hear, lamenting the sadness that the caged nightingale feels. The words of the song hung in the air like tears of crystal falling sadly into night.

The song finished and eventually he spoke, his back still to her. 'You did well not to interrupt me,' he said. 'I should have had you killed, and have thought no more about it. That is something to be sad about.' He turned, and they saw each other for the first time.

Prince Karim was handsome, as fine-featured and graceful as a stallion. Up until that moment he had merely known that something was missing in his life. But he saw the serving girl Ash El Dir and knew what it was that had been missing.

'You have brought me another birthday present?' he continued with a yawn, giving away no clue of his immense passion for her.

'Indeed, my lord,' said Ash, hoping that he would stop staring at her. 'It is a most rare treasure from the famous sailor Sindbad. I give it to you.' She produced the amulet of amethyst, and he marvelled at it.

'I have been sent so many presents by my father,' the Prince said, marvelling at the stone. 'Elephants and slaves, a coffin that no one can open, an ancient temple complete with priests, and an entire citadel that I shall never visit.'

'Then this stone cannot compete. If it does not please you, I shall return it.'

'On the contrary,' laughed the Prince, 'it pleases me. All the more because you bring it to me.'

Ash was confounded then, and, meaning to curse her misfortune, laughed.

The Prince laughed as well, and for a while no words passed between them.

'Look down from my balcony,' he said. 'For beyond us is the entire majesty of Baghdad, stretching out like the world. It is never quiet, some corner of it always surprises, and yet, wherever you hide, my father owns you. I stand and I look and I find it as beautiful as it is frightening.'

Ash stood by his side and, for a moment, forgot entirely about how she might win back the amethyst. 'The rarest of jewels is yours, my prince,' she said.

'Indeed, it is not,' said a voice. 'For it belongs to me.'

Standing in the air before them was the Wizard of Marabia, guardian of Egypt and the true ruler of the Nile. He was born aloft by knights of metal, carrying him onto the balcony before them as daintily as if he were a feather. Truly these were not just knights but also mighty Djinn.

Ash had never seen the Wizard of Marabia before, but she marvelled at his appearance. He was as tall as a lie, his eyes blazing. His face was hidden under his cowl, yet it was more that of a snarling beast than a creature of God.

'I am the Wizard of Marabia, and I have come for the amulet that this girl took from me.'

Prince Karim nodded. 'I accept your claim, of course, great wizard,' he said. 'But for one single point. The amulet is now the property of the mighty Caliph Haroun al-Raschid, and he has gifted it to me. Once something belongs to the Caliph, it is his for ever, and so I must, regretfully, deny it to you.'

Ash went to stand by the Prince's side.

He smiled at her. 'I shall protect you,' he told her.

She smiled back at him. 'It is I who shall protect you,' she said.

The Wizard of Marabia informed them he did not have time to dispute title, and instead ordered his mighty iron soldiers to kill them. Prince Karim discovered that it is one thing to shoot a frowsy peacock, another to injure a knight of iron. Instead it was the quick thinking and fast movements of Ash that protected them – once he swore he saw her pierced through by a blade, and yet she remained standing, beating back scimitars with candlesticks.

The Wizard stood watching the fight and laughing.

'I have guards, I have guards,' protested Prince Karim, 'and yet they do not come.'

'Maybe I have enchanted them asleep, maybe they do not like you,' proclaimed the Wizard. 'All that is between you and death is a girl. You should weep at that.'

'I do not weep,' the Prince told the Wizard. 'Instead I am both proud and grateful.'

'Yield, and you both shall live. I simply require the return of my amulet. I have hunted for it over the oceans far and wide ever since it was lost. It was only when this girl found it that I was able to locate it – she had a chance then to return it to me, and you are only in danger now because she disobeyed.'

'I am rather glad that she did,' the Prince told the Wizard. 'Otherwise I should not have met her.'

Ash had fought with the passion of an army, but her strength was finally waning. She turned to the Prince. 'My lord,' she said, 'would you like an adventure?'

'I am having an adventure.'

'Would you like more of an adventure?'

'Certainly.'

'Then, when I give the word, fetch that carpet from the wall.' Ash devoted herself to one of the metal knights, driving it back against the balcony wall. She drove her candlestick towards its face and the knight cried out, losing its balance and beginning to fall over the wall. As it toppled, she motioned to the Prince, and he threw the carpet over the metal knight. Both hung in the night sky. Ash jumped onto the carpet, and the Prince leapt up behind her.

'You have enchanted this carpet as much as me!' the Prince laughed as they slid away, over the palace, the domes and minarets and the waving roofs of the souk. 'Farewell, Wizard!'

Behind them the Wizard of Marabia raged – he would have pursued, but none of his soldiers was still standing. He cried after the two in tones of utter blackness. 'I am the Wizard of Marabia, the last true ruler of the Nile and I must have the amulet. Bring it to me.'

Instead, laughing, the two lovers flew off into the night.

And so paused the telling of the Lady Sherade.

The Lost Prince

Delighted by what he had heard, the Mighty King let Sherade live to tell another story. 'My lord,' she began, 'the clever servant girl Ash and Prince Karim had escaped from the mysterious Wizard of Marabia on a flying carpet…'

Ash El Dir and the Prince flew on, over cities and deserts, land and sea, until they came to a distant land. There they came to ground because the metal Djinn could fly no more. It lay under the carpet, no more than a heap of silver bones.

'I have never seen the like of it before,' said Prince Karim, but Ash was puzzled. She had seen the remains of such a creature in the crater on the cursed isle. Could it be that the amulet had really belonged once to the mysterious Wizard of Marabia?

'He seeks us still,' she told Prince Karim.

'As does my father,' Prince Karim laughed, kicking up the dust of the strange land. 'I wonder which of them I fear most? And yet here I am, with you on an adventure.'

'An adventure?' Ash looked dubiously around the desert.

'Why, yes.' Prince Karim smiled again. 'You've sailed with Sindbad, you've fought the Wizard of Marabia, you've plundered treasuries. More of that sort of thing.'

'To hear is to obey,' said Ash to the Prince. 'Did you bring any money with you?'

'No,' the Prince admitted. 'I did not think of that.'

'Then the next bit is going to be rather interesting for you.'

After a long walk and much careful endeavour, they managed to find humble lodgings in a small hovel. It was at the edge of a small town. There, Ash El Dir devoted herself to weaving intricate patterns of fabulous design which Karim was to sell in the market. Their lives were simple but happy. So much for them.

Meanwhile, the Wizard of Marabia sought for them high and low, in all the lands which the sky covered. He commanded great wealth and was able to buy his way into the minds of many, who swept across the deserts in a tide, looking for them.

At the same time, the Caliph of Baghdad was plunged into great lamentation at the loss of his favourite son.

'He has been stolen from you by a wicked Christian sorceress,' the Wizard informed the Caliph.

On hearing this, the Caliph ordered Sindbad dragged up from the deepest and darkest of the palace's many dungeons. 'Let a box be built for him at the gate of the principal mosque, and let the windows of the box be always open. There he shall sit, in the roughest garments, and order every Mussulman who passes into the mosque to spit in his face in passing. For so shall be punished those who conspire with infidel sorcerers.'

The Vizier saw that it was done, but Sindbad bore his punishment with such dignity that it was not long before he had won the sympathy of those that were best in the crowd. So much for him.

*

Meanwhile, in the distant land, Ash El Dir had guessed that the Wizard would be searching for them, and gave the following instructions to Prince Karim: 'Go out every day and sell my cloth on the markets. You may keep some of the money, but you must never use it to get drunk. Never boast about who you are, or how these fabrics are really woven. And never ever bring anyone back here, no matter how great a friend they are.'

'To hear is to obey,' Prince Karim smiled, and went off to the market.

For a long time he kept his word. In truth, he was happier than he could ever remember being in his life. The clever servant girl Ash was not just quick of hand and bright of looks, but she also entertained him truly. He, who had never needed a skill, discovered he was an honest and nimble salesman, and soon his fabrics were in high demand in the market, and he was selling whatever Ash could weave within a bare hour of arriving. This left him with time on his hands, and time is as great an enemy as it is a friend to man.

It was not long before Karim found a tavern on the edge of the market that was cool in the heat of the day. The food was rich, and the local wine even richer, but Karim remembered his promise to Ash El Dir, and only took a glass of it before heading home.

One day, an old man came up to him, wise of looks and bearing, and he complimented Karim on his manners and appearance. 'Sir, you are far superior to the normal merchant,' he greeted him.

Karim laughed, and began to tell him that he was not born a tradesman, then remembered his promise to Ash and left.

The next day, the same old man came up to him in the tavern again. This time he complimented him on his cloth. 'For a weaver, you have a grasp of patterns that is almost unique. Why, I've only seen the like on tabards worn by trading Norsemen.'

Karim expressed his surprise at this, and began to explain that he did not weave the patterns himself, and then he remembered his promise to Ash, and hurried home to her.

The third day, the old man came over to him again. 'My friend,' he said, 'I have brought you another cup of wine.' At first Karim refused, but the old man insisted. 'This is a very rare and expensive wine, and I would be most upset if it were to go to waste.'

Reluctantly, Karim reached out for it, and, in truth, it was excellent – both cold and yet fiery. 'I have not even drunk wine like this in my father's palace,' he told the old man, who appeared not to notice.

The two drank their wine, and then the old man pressed him to have another. 'For truly you are an excellent companion,' the old man said. 'Both regal and talented.'

They drank and talked long and late, until Karim remembered the time and vowed to return home. Somewhat unsteady of foot and mind, he allowed the old man to carry him there. At the last minute, he remembered his promise to Ash, and dismissed the old man hurriedly at his gate. He headed in, and the clever serving girl was much worried by his condition, but he shouted at her until she remembered her place and went back to her weaving.

The next day, Karim went to the market late, and was relieved not to find the old man in the tavern. Once he had eaten a simple lunch, he went home to the loyal serving girl, meaning to apologise to her. But he found her gone, the house empty. He knew then that, through his own foolishness, he had lost both his happiness and his love.

After much lamentation and incomprehension, he searched the house and found a note concealed in her pillow. 'Oh Karim, heart and life, when you came home last night, I knew that you had fallen into the hands of deceivers. I have noticed the amount that you come home with falling every day, and I had hoped that you had remembered your promises to me. But I saw the old man lurking outside last night, and I saw him again this morning. He can be nothing but an agent of the Wizard of Marabia. Do not blame yourself for what you have done, for you are simply a man, although I know that you will blame yourself, also because you are a man. If you find this note, both I and the amulet will have been taken to the Wizard. I have kept back and hidden some money at the bottom of this pillowcase, and I hope that you will use it either to make your way home or to come and find me – whichever way your heart leads you.'

When Karim read this he fell fully into despair and lamentation and wished he was dead. For he had lost all he valued, and had simply an empty house. He knew now how much he loved the serving girl Ash El Dir, and how much he wished to be reunited with her. But beyond the town was desert. How was he to find her?

And so paused the telling of the Lady Sherade.

The Finding of the King

Delighted by what he had heard, the mighty King let Sherade live to continue the story.

'Will there be a happy ending? Will the lovers be reunited? Will the Prince learn the error of his ways? And what of the Wizard of Marabia?'

'All will be explained, my husband,' the Lady Sherade assured him. 'For many days and many nights, Prince Karim wandered the empty lands looking for his lost love, the clever servant girl Ash El Dir…'

Eventually, he came to a fabulous city of shining marble overlooking a harbour of the deepest blue. Most places he had travelled through he had been treated most unlike a prince. He had been turned from the walls and had dirt thrown at him, but here he received true hospitality.

One of the Vizier's servants bade him enter a courtyard, and offered him a new set of clothes in return for his old ones. But Karim refused. 'These clothes, poor though they now are, were made for me by my one true love. I have lost her, and these are all I have of her.'

The Vizier's man said he understood and asked for them again, promising to do what could be done to wash and mend them. Not trusting him, and full of sorrow for the state he was in, Karim refused. The man nodded, and told him to sit at the back of the courtyard, in the shadows.

In the centre of the courtyard was a big fountain, flowing with clear water, and cups were handed out to several hundred travellers, all dressed in clean white linen. Great bowls of rice were brought out for them, along with meat and fruit. There was plenty to go round at this feast of beggars.

Karim hung back, and a maid brought over a tin bowl of water and a thin plate of rice, and Karim ate it in the shadows of the courtyard, like a low dog. He no longer resented the loss of his palace, or wished to return to the splendours of Baghdad. He simply embraced his lowly position as all that he deserved. Indeed, starving though he was, he did not eat all of his food. While the other supplicants cleared their plates, he ate but half and then asked if there was someone more deserving of his portion.

With a trumpet and cheering, the King of the City of Marble appeared on a platform. He was very young and very handsome, and he surveyed the supplicants with kind eyes. All of them muttered a grateful obeisance.

The Vizier announced, 'It is His Majesty's pleasure to see that he has fed the wandering poor. He feeds those without food, he clothes those who need to cover their backs. He wishes no man to wander the desert without protection.'

The crowd nodded and cheered.

The Vizier continued: 'And sometimes, our Great King singles out some for preferment if they be especially deserving.'

The crowd cheered more and sat up straight, running their hands through their hair to make the most of themselves.

The silent, handsome young King surveyed the crowd and then stopped. 'There is one here I like,' he said.

The supplicants looked from one to the other, curious, eager and sly. Each knew in his heart of hearts that it was him.

The King pointed. 'What's he that sits in the shadows like a chastened dog? Bring him forward.'

The Vizier's guards dragged Karim through the crowd, who looked at him and marvelled. What had he done to deserve such favour? He had not even changed out of his rags.

'Who are you, stranger? Speak,' the King commanded.

Karim spoke low, not looking the King in the eyes. 'I am not deserving of your notice. I have lost all that I hold dear.'

'All that you hold dear? Were you once rich? Were you once powerful?'

'Aye, I was all that. But that matters not. I lost all that I loved because I did not heed her advice.'

'I see,' the King said. 'It is easily done,' he laughed, and his courtiers laughed with him, and nudged each other.

'Why do you single me out, your majesty? I have fed, and I am grateful. Please, let me slink back into my shadows.'

'I have singled you out…' The King paused. 'Because you are thinner than the rest.' He smiled. In truth, a lot of the supplicants were not begging travellers, but lived happily in the city and came here for a free meal. The King turned to his Vizier. 'Take this man to my chambers. I shall visit him later. Once you have bathed him.'

Karim was dragged away, protesting. He heard the King's high laugh and the muttering of the other supplicants.

Prince Karim was taken to sumptuous rooms that smelt of lemon. A host of handsome young men came for him. A bath was drawn for him, full of unguents. His clothes were wrested from him, and washed where he could see them, and then, after he had been shaved, he allowed himself to be lowered into the hot waters of the bath.

He looked around, at the many handsome youths, and he felt a fear gather inside him for the nature of the gift that the King intended to bestow on him. He felt worried, but the bath was hot, and he fell fast asleep.

When he woke up the water had gone, and he was lying down on a bed. There came a laugh from behind him, and he realised he was naked. He looked around for his clothes, but could not see them.

'Oh, fool that I was to be parted from them!' he wailed.

'Fool that you were,' laughed the King's voice. 'No, don't turn around. I wish to see you like this.'

'Oh, your majesty, I would not have you see me like this.'

'On the contrary,' the King laughed, coming closer. 'I would see more of you exactly like this.'

'There is some mistake,' protested Karim. 'My heart belongs to another.'

'But your body now belongs to me,' the King said. He laughed again, and something landed on the bed. Karim looked at it. They were his clothes, washed, dried and marvellously mended. He stared at them.

'If they were so precious to you, why did you let them be taken from you?' asked the King.

Karim had no answer. He beheld his clothes, and he wept.

'Would you still look at those rags?' asked the King. 'Or would you look at me? I who have fed you, bathed you, shown you kindness, and intend to do much for you?'

Reluctantly, Prince Karim turned away from the garments, and instead faced the King.

The King was smiling, his handsome face dancing, as first he took off his crown, then he laid aside his cape, and finally, he took off his beard.

Prince Karim was amazed.

Standing laughing at him was Ash El Dir.

The lovers were reunited, and in their rejoicing there was no pain, no guilt, no sorrow. Ash El Dir told Karim that, realising the agents of the Wizard had found them, there was nothing to do.

'While you used your savings from my earnings on pleasant things—'

'That's unfair.'

'Is it? I am King here. Think carefully…'

'It was fair. Tell me.'

'As long as we held the amulet, they would know the region in which we were. It was only a matter of time,' she told him…

The Hiding of the Amulet

And so Ash El Dir told him of how, as long as she and Prince Karim had the amulet, it was only a matter of time before the Wizard of Marabia found them…

I used what I had to pay for our rent, to feed us, and to buy materials. With many of them I wove, but I also bought sheets of lead and paid a casket-maker to fashion two caskets, one to fit in the other. This I concealed the amulet in. For I remembered the Wizard had only been able to sense the amulet when I had fetched it from the crater. So, it needed to be hidden from the air. Alas, the caskets were hardly finished before you betrayed us to the agents of the Wizard. I tried to flee, but the old man caught me, and dragged me out into the desert, away from all I loved. We travelled on for forty days and nights, the old man never speaking, just pulling me on until his mules died, then we walked, walked into the sands.

Finally the old man spoke to me. And this is what he said: 'This body has been given to the Wizard of Marabia, last and truest ruler of the Nile. This body has been given to him entirely and now it is empty. More hosts are coming and they will find you. They are very close. Do not think to run, for now it is time for you to carry my master's spirit for a while.' So saying, the light went out of the old man's eyes and he died, becoming the dust as he fell into it.

All was peace, and then I felt something looking through my eyes – a shadow as dark and old as the night sky. I could feel its hunger as it prowled my head like a ravenous dog. For a moment, we were evenly matched and then it pounced. I have never felt more alone and more lost than at that instant, and then I did truly despair. But I woke up in the sand, my mouth dry, and an echo in my head. 'There is no home for me here. But I shall find you.'

I knew then that I had escaped. Looking onto the horizon, I could see dust kicked up by riders, and I knew I did not have long. I ran through the sands until they became the parched weeds of scrubland. A town was nearby, but the riders were closer. I covered myself in sand, burying the casket with me, and waited. The heat was unbearable, the sand as hot as the Sultan's finest oven, but I waited until the riders had passed – I knew they would search the town. Tempting as it was to follow them, I skirted the town, eating weeds and drinking what water I could find, until I discovered a barn, and crept into a cart of straw. And then I slept the sleep of those who God has turned away from.

When I awoke, I was bumping up and down. The cart was under way. I looked around.

'So you've awoken?'

It was an old farmer. She had found me and, realising me a fugitive or beggar, had taken me with her on her journey. She had fresh milk and cheese for me, and was kindness itself. She had lived alone for many years, and said she would value the company on the long journey to the Marble City. 'The roads are not safe for women on their own, after all. Many are the devils and ruffians who may assault us,' the old woman said and laughed.

I told her my story and she listened with patience and kindness. 'Then you will find welcome in the Marble City. The King there had three sons and they long ago went on a quest to find the fabled City of Brass. None returned, but he puts food out every day for the poor in case one of them is his son returning.'

I left the old farmer and went to the palace where food was laid out. I had disguised myself as a man as best as I could, and, before I knew where life went, I had attracted the attention of a fine lady. She had me presented to her in her apartments, much as I summoned you. She was the King's daughter. He had forbidden her to go on the quest for the City of Brass, and she had remained here.

'Daughters do not get to go on quests,' the Princess Zubaida lamented. 'If they did, I am sure my brothers would not have been lost. And now, alas, my father is preparing to sit down with the Destroyer of Delights. When he departs, the kingdom will fall. Unless, that is, I marry.' And the Princess smiled at me. 'You have a bearing about you. Will you marry me?'

I explained the truth of who I was, and she laughed. 'That matters not a fig,' she said. 'All I want is someone who can counterfeit being a lost prince.'

And so I was presented to the King as the questing Prince Karim, son of the Caliph Haroun al-Raschid of Baghdad. No, don't interrupt, my love, for this is my story.

The King and the Vizier examined me in many matters of philosophy and mathematics, science and literature, and I was able to satisfy all of them.

'Truly,' the Old King said to Princess Zubaida, 'this is a prince wise far beyond his years. You have chosen wisely.' And so saying, he kissed her cheeks and went out onto the terrace to look at his kingdom while he awaited the arrival of the Destroyer of Delights.

Queen Zubaida and I have reigned ever since. I have continued the tradition of the greeting of travelling strangers in the hopes that one day you would be, by the kindness of God, returned to me. And the Queen has devoted herself to statehood with all the brilliance of her father, mixed with the kindness and infinite patience that only a sister of brothers can have.

And now, my love, you are here, so the time has come to resume our quest. For a long time have I searched for the City of Brass, and these people have many maps and charts. Many have set out there from here. But none have returned…

'You cannot stop there!' protested the King, as the Lady Sherade paused in her story.

'I was worried, my husband, that I was fatiguing you. After all, the hour is late, and the leisure of a mighty King is precious.'

The King begged her to continue.

The City of Brass

'Long and hard did Ash El Dir and Prince Karim seek for the City of Brass,' continued the Lady Sherade. 'The maps of the Marble Kingdom were good, but the way was perilous…'

In truth they lost many of their retinue, many noble knights simply turning back to the city. This in many ways suited the Ash El Dir and Prince Karim. 'The City of Brass is only for the bravest and the truest,' said Ash El Dir.

'But what is it? And how does the amulet help?'

'That I do not entirely know,' admitted Ash El Dir. 'The world is strange and no man can know all. And yet without the amulet no one can be admitted to the City of Brass. And without entering the City of Brass, no one can know what is inside it.'

'I have heard the knights talk of great riches,' said Prince Karim, and he spurred his horse on.

'Riches are not all, my prince,' laughed Ash El Dir.

They passed at length a temple, with a flame forever burning from the centre of the earth. An inscription was carved at the gateway to the flame: 'This burns for the memory of the 750 gods who fell. This burns for the memory of those several thousand who sought the City of Brass and perished.' At this sight, many of the remaining knights turned back.

Ash and Karim and a bare handful of knights continued on, crossing the wastes between Araby and Egypt. Lying in their way was a vast stone creature, part lion and part woman.

'I fought in the great battle of the gods, and I was on the losing side. It is now my punishment to wait for travellers such as you,' the Sphinx said. 'I offer a last warning to all those who seek the City of Brass. Be prepared to lose all that you hold dear. Many thousand thousand have lost their lives.'

'I do not fear to lose my life,' said Ash El Dir, and the Sphinx laughed.

'Then what else have you to lose?'

At that, three more of the party set on their sad way home. Two men only stayed with them, talking all the way of the pleasures that lay ahead of them in the red lands between Araby and Thebes.

Shimmering on the horizon were the walls of a great city – not brass but stone.

'Can this be the brass city?' said Karim. 'I see no brass.'

They walked the vast stone walls and there was no entrance in sight. All was quiet. In the high sky, brightly plumed birds wheeled overhead.

'We must climb the walls,' ventured the men, and Karim agreed with them. Ash El Dir urged caution, but one of the men fashioned a ladder, and scrambled up to the top of the wall.

'What can you see?' they asked him.

'I can see Paradise,' he cried with delight. 'I can see the beauty and I cannot wait.' So saying he dived from the wall into the city. They heard his joyful cry cut short.

'This is not right,' declared Ash El Dir, but the other man was already clambering the ladder and would not listen to caution. He too declared that he saw Paradise. He started to describe the quenching of all thirsts, but he too dived joyously from the walls into the space beyond, and was heard from no more.

Prince Karim also made to scale the ladder, but Ash El Dir tethered him firmly to it. 'Just in case there is no paradise beyond.'

Prince Karim reached the mighty battlements, and called down to her in delight. 'Truly, my love, there is all that man could wish for. A beautiful lake, crystal waters shimmering in the sun.'

'Where are our fellows? What has happened to them?' she asked, but he did not listen. He had already dived from the walls.

The tether caught him, and Ash held the ladder as his joyous shouts became a scream.

'Help me, oh, help me,' cried Prince Karim.

'What has happened?' called Ash, climbing the ladder to hold the tether.

'Do not come onto the walls – for you will see a lake so pure it has to be dived into. Fool that I am, I wished to swim in it, but no sooner had I jumped than the lake vanished and I found myself falling onto stone. Help me, I beg of you.'

At length, and with difficulty, Ash El Dir fetched Karim back up, until he lay on the parapet once more. 'I can see the lake again. Perhaps it is no mirage,' he called, and made to dive again, but Ash jerked him back onto the ladder.

They climbed down and Prince Karim looked up at the great stone walls again. 'Perhaps, the warnings are true – only the dead can enter the City of Brass.'

'Or maybe it is where the amulet is to earn its value,' said Ash El Dir. She produced the caskets, unlocking them. 'The amethyst belongs to the city. It is said that none can be admitted without it. Perhaps it is the key to it. No wonder the Wizard of Marabia seeks it.' She opened the casket, full knowing that once she did so, the Wizard would be able to sense the amethyst. 'We must try.'

They walked around the long walls three times, pressing the amethyst against the walls and hoping. Incredibly, there were no gaps, no breaks, no joins between the stones.

'Perhaps this is not even the City of Brass,' scoffed Karim, but Ash walked on.

'The lesson is time,' she said. 'There is a gap, but it has taken us time to see it – there.'

And so saying, she pushed the amethyst into the tiniest of gaps that had never been there before.

'Open Sesame,' announced Ash. Karim had never heard this before and questioned her of it. 'Oh, it is the password for the secret cave of the Guild of Thieves.'

'Not very memorable.'

'Really?'

As they spoke, the gateway to the great stone wall appeared.

'To see is to obey,' said Ash El Dir, and they went inside…

And here the Lady Sherade would have paused her story, but the mighty King her husband pressed her to continue.

Inside the vast stone walls was a sumptuous plain containing the real City of Brass – lofty palaces, splendid domes, splendid mansions – all of brass, and all of a unique design, the like of which no living man had seen. Every feature glowed marvellous ruddy hues under the favour of the sun. Ash El Dir was moved to tears and Karim was silent with awe.

'What wealth can the Caliph of this city have?' he marvelled.

Ash shook her head. 'Listen to the city – it is silent,' she said. 'The City of Brass sleeps.'

They walked on through, past the gates and into the empty streets. Their echoing footsteps were the only noise apart from the birds wheeling overhead. They came to a market, where the canopied stalls fluttered in the breeze. The stallholders were still there, frozen as if selling their wares, but the comfort of death had long ago embraced them.

'What happened here?' asked Ash, fingering the wonderful cloth. They walked on, into a vast square in which sheets of copper had been beaten till veined like marble. Crowded into a corner of the square, as though frozen in the act of trying to run away, were more bodies, their skin blackened and shrunk around the bones. They made the same finding in the houses, the libraries and the schools. Everyone in this fine city had perished.

They entered the grandest palace of all, making their way past scores of fallen soldiers. The walls of the palace were decorated even more richly, and Karim marvelled at the jewel-danced carvings, depicting a fearsome figure – the Goddess None Dare Fight.

'Zekahmet – I have never heard of her,' said Karim.

'Maybe her religion is so old it has been forgotten,' Ash suggested, for she was as wise as she was clever.

They pressed on into the heart of the palace, and found there the figure of a Queen. Even in death, the figure was beautiful, her elegant hands still gripping the arms of her throne.

'Even though she has burned, her eyes are still like jewels.' Karim bowed to the still regal figure.

'It is as though a fire has swept through the City of Brass, putting to death all the citizens, but left the buildings untouched. What flame can do that?'

'It is the work of Djinns,' pronounced the Prince, for he knew much of magic. 'I wager this is the Wizard of Marabia.'

'If that was so, why sought he the key?' asked Ash.

'I sought the key because I wished to come home,' said the Wizard. For he now stood behind them.

And so paused the Lady Sherade.

The Confrontation in the City of Brass

'The Wizard of Marabia had found Prince Karim and the clever servant Ash El Dir in the City of Brass, where the buildings and the dead waited silently,' continued the Lady Sherade.

The Wizard of Marabia confronted them, his mighty Djinns floated behind him. He smiled a smile that was clever and sad. 'If you would not give me the key, I decided to wait until you used it. I have got what I came for – I have come home.'

Karim then rounded on him, accusing him of all the felonies under the night. 'These bodies? Did you kill them all?'

'Ah, alas, no,' the Wizard sighed, and one of his metal knights held him up. 'These poor figures, these were my dearest friends. And that figure on the throne – she is my one true Queen. The Goddess Zekahmet. Yea, I claim title as the last and truest ruler of the Nile, but I do so on her behalf. For she is the Goddess of Fire and Vengeance.'

'What happened here?' asked Ash El Dir.

'Fire and Vengeance…' began the Wizard. 'It is a sad story…'

The Wizard of Marabia's Story

Even longer ago than in ancient time, *began the Wizard,* man walked the Earth as little more than the beasts. Then, just as we began to look up at the heavens, travellers came down from them. They were not men such as us. They came from other spheres and realms, places of magic and metal. We called them gods, and they did not deny it – they had knowledge and power we could hardly dream of. As they walked the Earth, they raised great buildings, they inspired artists with their visions, and they changed everyone they met.

Some ran screaming in fear from them, some ran adoringly towards them. Tribes raised armies against them which they smote unto dust. Great kings sought to marry their daughters to them. Thinkers ran to them demanding answers to great questions, and medics begged them for cures. We were swift to embrace these gods because, like wise parents, they told us what to do. We were slow to realise that the gods childishly fought among themselves. We thought them perfect, each and every one, but they differed and they argued. Some did not talk to each other, some declared that the world would be destroyed unless another of their kind was killed, and so, as rich as life became, it also waxed more complicated.

Mightier battles were fought with greater weapons than had ever been wielded before. Soldiers died in the thousand thousand, and kingdoms burned. One god rose up against his brothers and nearly destroyed them all. After he was vanquished, it was announced that the Great Gods of Egypt would leave. Their time was over.

But what of us? Those of us who had slaved in the houses of the gods as their faithful priests and servants? What was to become of us? We could not return to our people – if our gods were gone, they would surely kill us. One god remained – Zekahmet, in her City of Brass. A sanctuary that would shield us all from the world. A place that would remain the same. She vowed that she would protect us from her brethren. For she was as vengeful as she was graceful. She treated us like her pets – those birds that turn above us in the sky are no mere carrion, they are the remains of the noble-plumed birds that paraded in her courtyards. Zekahmet loved beauty and peace. She built a heaven on this Earth, a garden protected from outside where she could be worshipped and we could enjoy her protection for ever.

Her brethren found out about her desertion, and there was wrath in the skies. They quested over every land, looking for the City of Brass, but we evaded them for a long time. Then they found its region, and the last battle began. They could never find the precise location, they could never get inside the City itself, although they enlisted the very worst of men to help – the Ancient Guild of Thieves worked day and night to find every scrap about the City. But the whereabouts of the City, even the sight of its great impregnable walls, remained closed to them.

And then, one day, I betrayed my great Queen. I did not mean to. My metal Djinns and I had been out on patrol when thieves ambushed me. I escaped, but I did not realise that I brought an Ifrit back with me – a treacherous creature which reported the location and the way into the City of Brass.

No sooner had I made my way into the throne room to report victory to my great Queen than the Ifrit appeared from my back and bowed to Zekahmet.

'Oh great Queen, great Goddess, all is lost to you because you trusted this man. For man is a fool and not worthy of you. It is all over for you now.'

I protested my innocence, but my Queen turned to me and nodded. 'Go. You are exiled from this city. You have not the honour to die amongst us.'

I fled, fled with my knights, sailing away in my flying iron galleon. I vowed I would fight off the attack from the other gods. We would save the City of Brass. But it was not to be. The weapon they used was so mighty and so quick – little more than a flash and the very air was torn asunder. I heard my Queen's scream, and I knew the Goddess was no more. That was the last moment of happiness I enjoyed, for the great weapon touched even my galleon, casting it into the ground. My Djinn saved me, but the galleon was lost, I knew not where, its location hidden by our enemies.

I walked the world for ever, carrying my heaviest burden. For Zekahmet would not let me die – you cannot know the torment it is being unable to die. Oh, young girl, you laugh at me now, but the pain knows no boundaries and the weight of the years is terrible indeed to carry.

And that is why I sought out the location of the amethyst key. I had long forgotten it. For hundreds of years I wandered this Earth until the sand became dust. I saw the terrible effects of that weapon become reflected in the many lands. Peoples whose minds were pulled inside out, who could conjure great feats but could not talk, animals grown to great size or able to converse. Although I did not know where my original galleon had fallen to the ground, although my Djinn scoured the realms for signs of its passing, I still hoped to find it. If my amulet had survived, then my chances of regaining the City were there.

I know why you seek this place – the young man seeks wealth and power. The young woman seeks escape. There is no escape from the City of Brass. It always was, in a way, a prison. I have come back here because it is the only place under the skies where I can die. Take what you want from this kingdom – the people who delighted in the City's joys have passed. Take what you want, I say again, only leave my Queen's body alone. She gave herself to try and save us all, and she will for ever remain holy.

Now I feel my breathing tighten, and I know that the Sunderer of Companions comes to visit me at last. And so I end my days.

The End of the City of Brass

With that, the Wizard of Marabia closed his eyes, and his metal knights held him aloft, placing him on a bier which they stood guard around.

Ash El Dir looked around piteously, crying for herself and for the city. 'There is no escape. This is an empty quest. A failure.'

'How can you say that?' Prince Karim upbraided her. 'There is so much wealth here! So many wonders! We have a greater treasury here than any of your Ancient Guild of Thieves.' So saying he began to gather in his arms the riches of the City of Brass, plucking precious stones from the walls and stuffing fabrics of spun gold into his sack.

Ash El Dir begged him to cease, but he shook his head. 'Your friend the Wizard has ordered us to. And I merely obey.' He pulled at a necklace worn by the Goddess Zekahmet, but Ash stayed him. 'You cannot, that is forbidden.'

The Prince nodded, and agreed. 'You are wise. It is forbidden,' he said, and then he changed his mind. 'It is so, and yet, it is not a thing that she may enjoy more.' He tugged the necklace from her throat. For a moment, it seemed as though the Goddess smiled at him, and then her figure crumbled away. And with her fading, the City of her dreams began to shake, its minarets and spires falling apart.

'She sustained it! Only she,' cursed Ash El Dir. 'Had you left her be, this would have been yours to enjoy for ever.'

And Karim burst out wailing, begging her to stop it.

'But there is nothing I can do, not against the last wishes of a god.'

In despair and panic Karim ran away, fleeing outside, gathering up all the gold and jewels he could as he went.

Ash El Dir stood in the throne room. This was, she thought, as good a place, as noble a dwelling to die as any. Perhaps, in many ways, the best option she would have. She went over to the Wizard of Marabia, and stroked his cheek. Then bowing to the dust of the Queen, she left to continue life.

Stood out on the sands of the great plain, all she could hear behind her was the roar as the mighty City of Brass collapsed. Metal shrieked against metal, and stone split against stone. Palaces, fountains, libraries and treasuries all shimmered and vanished. Ash El Dir stood until all was silence. Behind her were the great walls, with nothing beyond them.

In front of her was nothing. Prince Karim had not waited. Either through fear or hatred, the love of her life had left her. He had taken his vast riches and run.

All that was left for her were the birds wheeling overhead, calling to each other in grief at the end of the City of Brass.

There the Lady Sherade stopped.

'Is that really how it ends?' gasped the Mighty King.

The Lady Sherade laughed.

'But what of Sindbad, left in his box?'

'So much for him, I told you, and so much for him.'

'That is not enough!' protested the King. 'I wish for his story to have an ending.'

The Lady Sherade considered. 'Then perhaps he stayed in his box until Ash El Dir returned and released him and the people were full sorry and marvelled at what she said and the Caliph bestowed on everyone his munificence.'

'That is better.'

'Or perhaps she forgot all about him and walked on in the world.'

'That is not.'

The Lady Sherade shrugged. 'Is that all you want to know – if maybe there is some of this story which I have left out?'

'Ash El Dir – the clever serving girl. She did not get her rewards, did she?'

'No,' Lady Sherade agreed. 'She did not become rich, she did not travel to the heavens, and the love of her life,

the man who she had hoped to spend her days with in perfect happiness until he was visited by the Destroyer of Delights – he abandoned her and never thought of her again. That is a knowledge that is hard to live with, however long your life is.'

'Well, yes, poor thing,' admitted the King. 'But a serving girl marry a king? That only happens in fairy stories, such as you spin, my Queen. I find it fascinating that you tell me such things, though. I had heard such legends of my grandfather Karim, but I had never dreamt the full story was so exciting – it is, of course, all invention, but how pleasant.'

'Is that all you think the story is?' the Lady Sherade teased her new husband.

Laughing, he embraced her. 'Of course not! It is full of pretty words so very entertaining that they have kept you alive, and I am very glad of that.' He smiled and she smiled back. He broke away and took another glass of sherbet.

'Is there no more to my words than that, my lord?'

He considered the cup of sherbet. 'Your tales are like this drink – a sweet and amusing concoction. Once one has begun, one cannot cease.' He filled the cup and drank again. 'You are most gifted.'

'What did you think of my characters?'

'Oh most vivid, most vivid. As though you'd met them.' He nudged his wife in the ribs. 'Come though, we must have a happier ending to your last tale.'

'Indeed we must.' She tipped the lees of the jug into his glass. 'I shall tell you one thing first. My stories had a motto – a common theme, whether fact or fable, that every man should listen to.'

'Tell me, what is it?' said the King, tapping her on the nose.

She stood then, bowing before him. He made to embrace her, but try as he might, he could not move. Gasping in surprise, he tried to call for help, but no voice had he. Instead he lay there on the couch, and he was not alone. The Destroyer of Delights had come to visit him.

As he drew his last choking breath, he heard the laugh of Lady Sherade. 'Husband, my moral is this… You are always better off with a Queen than a King…'

The Fortunate Isles

David Llewellyn

1

Letting go of the rope she fell, hitting the ground hard, and tumbled forward, grazing her hands against the cobbled street. No time to feel sorry for herself. Scrambling to her feet and clapping the stones and grit from her palms, Ash began to run. Already, she could hear armed guards and bloodhounds pouring from the castle gates and – from a window high above – the Princess, high-pitched and nasal, shrieking, 'Stop her! Stop the thief!'

On this moonless night in 1485, the city of Seville was like an ants' nest; a maze of manmade gullies and canyons in which it was easy to get lost. Ramshackle, timber-framed buildings jostled one another for space, darkening the streets and alleyways, but Ash – an old, young woman once named Ashildr – had memorised her route, each twist and turn from the castle to the port, and could have made her way there blindfolded if she had to.

She ran and ran and zigged and zagged till the *clump-clump-clump* of the guards and barking of their dogs faded away, and she had only the echo of her own footsteps for company. Presently, having reached the port, she stopped running and edged her way carefully and silently along the quayside, hidden by the shadows. There, bobbing gently in the dim harbour lights, was a carrack with the name *El Galgo – The Greyhound* – painted across its stern. Preparations were being made, a steady column of men carrying crates and cages up its gangplank, the decks bustling with activity. Bound, no doubt, for Genoa or Marseilles.

It was perfect.

Pulling her cap a little lower over her brow and hoisting one of the crates up against her chest, Ash marched straight onto the *Galgo*, as if she had every right to be there. Then, sneaking away from the crew, she began searching for a place to stow away, and found one below decks, in a room already filled with sacks of rice, beans and flour, barrels of anchovies and honey, pipes and butts of wine and stocks of pickled pork. Though cramped, its far corner had just enough room for her to hide, and she doubted even the ship's cook would notice if she borrowed one or two supplies during the voyage.

Hunkering down in the shadows, on a makeshift bed of flour sacks, Ash took the lizard brooch from her pocket, careful not to snag her thumb on its pointed tail, and she tilted it this way and that, so that its emerald scales and ruby eyes glistened in what little light there was.

Ugly little thing, really. Oh, Ash knew it was meant to be priceless and that its maker was considered a genius in his own lifetime, but *really*. Some people had more money than taste. Still, if the Condottiero in Pisa wanted this brooch for his mistress and was willing to pay two thousand ducats to have it stolen, who was she to quibble?

Ash put the brooch away and tried to sleep, but it was no use. Her 'bed' was not exactly comfortable, and her thoughts were restless with too many 'hows' and 'what ifs' and the melody of a madrigal she'd heard in Paris several months ago and simply couldn't forget, however hard she tried.

At first light, the *Galgo* left the port of Seville and made its way slowly – too slowly, for Ash's liking – along the winding River Guadalquivir. Her view of the world outside came through a grille in the ceiling, offering only a latticed blue square of sky. She listened out for the voices of the crew, but still couldn't gather where they were bound, and it was many hours before she heard the cawing of seagulls and the waves that seemed to shush them, and knew that they were finally at sea.

11

Five days in and they were still sailing west. How did she know this? Because each day, as she hid away in that dark corner of the hold, the sunlight coming through the grille came only from the starboard side. But what lay to the west of Seville? There were the Azores, the Portuguese islands, but why would any Spanish ship go *there*?

She'd done a good job of hiding so far – keeping as quiet as a mouse whenever anyone came into the hold, stealing only tiny morsels of food, and answering nature's call in the dead of night when most of the crew were asleep – but she wasn't sure she could keep it up much longer. Ash had chosen the *Galgo* because it was a Spanish ship, because she'd assumed it might be bound for somewhere not too far away, some port that would get her that little bit closer to the Condottiero's palace. It seemed she was very much mistaken.

Maybe it was the lack of sleep that clouded her judgement, or her impatience and curiosity simply got the better of her, but on the fifth day, when the decks were at their busiest, Ash left the hold and stepped out into the midmorning light. After all, she reasoned, the *Galgo* must have a complement of forty crew. Impossible for anyone to know *everyone* on board…

But she was wrong.

No sooner had she reached the deck than a big, booming voice yelled, 'Who in blazes are you?'

The speaker was a titan, a man who towered over her, eclipsing the sun, his face hidden behind a bushy black beard and a scarlet eyepatch.

'My name's Ash, sir. I'm the… cabin boy?'

The giant whisked away her cap and roared with laughter. 'Cabin boy?' he said. 'Pull the other one, miss! Looks like we've got ourselves a stowaway, lads!'

Ash was surrounded. This, then, was how it would end. This time. Thrown overboard to be eaten by sharks. That was a new one. She wondered briefly how it might feel, and how long it would take her to mend afterwards. That was assuming she *could* mend after passing through the digestive system of a shark…

'I'm *very* sorry,' she said, hoping it would be enough, but knowing it wouldn't.

'She's sorry, lads,' said the giant. 'Do I accept her apology? Or do I kick her backside in the briny blue?'

Among a chorus of men shouting, 'Kick her in the sea!' someone emerged from the crowd; a tall, thin man dressed more elegantly than the rest, with dark brown hair and a reddish beard.

'Are you really proposing we kill this girl?' he said.

'That's what's done with stowaways,' said the giant, who Ash now took to be the captain.

'Hardly an auspicious start, though, is it?'

'Then what do you suggest?'

'That we find something for her to do?'

The giant glowered down at Ash. 'Well, girl. What are you good at? Do you sew?'

Ash made a face and shook her head.

'Cook? Clean?'

She shook her head again.

'See? She's useless.'

'I'm good with a sword.'

The giant laughed. 'Oh, really? Hear that, lads? She's good with a sword!' Then he turned to one of his crew, a scrawny-looking character with one eyebrow, and said: 'Fernando. Give the girl your cutlass.'

Hesitantly, this Fernando stepped forward and passed her his sword, giving Ash a look halfway between distrust and sympathy.

'Now, then,' bellowed the giant. 'Let's see what you're made of, shall—'

Before he could finish his sentence the cutlass whistled through the air, the tip of its blade passing mere inches from his throat, and the lower part of his beard rained down around his feet in a shower of black tufts. A deathly silence fell across the deck, and the giant reached up, probing his now beardless chin with an expression of alarm. Just as Ash began to fear the worst, he laughed.

'Oh, I like her,' he said. 'She can stay.'

Then with a hefty right hook, he punched her in the face, and her bright blue day turned instantly to night.

III

The thin man with the red beard was the ship's physician, Garcia, and he was the first person Ash saw, when she came to in a room below deck. There, he explained everything. The giant whose beard she'd clipped was, indeed, the ship's captain, Francisco Lopez, and there was a very good reason the *Galgo* was sailing west, out into the ocean.

They were engaged in a race with a Genoese ship named the *San Giorgio*, both of them searching for a western route to Asia. For years, the Mamluk and Ottoman Sultans in Egypt and Turkey had made the old land routes, the ones traversed by Marco Polo and his brothers, impassable. To reach India, China or Japan you would have to sail either around Africa's Cape of Good Hope, which no European had ever done, or west across the Atlantic, and into the unknown.

Ash's timing, Garcia told her, was impeccable. Since leaving Seville, they'd discovered that the ship's lookout, a rather timid lad named Diego, suffered terribly from a fear of heights, and few others on board were nimble enough to climb up to the crow's nest. While she was unconscious, Captain Lopez had decided to make Ash the new lookout.

From that day on, the hours she spent, suspended high above the deck, were long and tedious, and, though she was grateful Lopez and his men hadn't thrown her to the sharks, Ash still wondered if she would ever find her way back to her client, the Condottiero, and her two thousand ducats.

Nine days into the voyage, they stopped on the island of São Miguel – as far as anyone knew, one of the last bits of dry land between Europe and distant China – to carry out repairs to the ship and replenish their supply of fresh water. Then they set sail once more, and Ash was back in the crow's nest, staring out at the boundless deep blue void. Once or twice she saw whales breach the surface, firing great spumes of foam up into the air before diving back beneath the waves, but more often than not it was as if they had entered a part of the world where no other living creature dared to roam.

IV

It was on the twentieth day that she saw it: the *San Giorgio*. Just a grey silhouette at first; then, as they drew nearer, the red crosses of St George visible on its flag and sails. She called out to the Captain, and Lopez had his crew man every station, preparing the cannons in case it was some sort of trap.

As they drew closer still, Ash saw a single person moving about on the *San Giorgio*'s deck, a handsome man only a little older than herself, waving at them with his chaperon hat in his hand. Finally, when the two ships were only feet apart, and before Lopez and his men could board the *San Giorgio*, the stranger came rushing across the gangplank crying, 'Thank you! Oh, Lord be praised! It is a miracle!'

Then, overcome with happiness or exhaustion, he collapsed.

While Lopez and his men began searching the *San Giorgio*, Ash helped Garcia carry the Genoese stranger below deck, and moments later he came around, blinking up at them in wonder as if they might be angels. Garcia held a cup of water to the stranger's lips, helping him to drink, and asked him his name.

'Piero of Lodi,' the stranger replied. 'Emissary of his Grace, Gian Galleazzo, Duke of Milan.'

'But what happened?' asked Ash. 'Where is everyone?'

Piero's expression darkened. 'They are dead,' he replied. 'They are all dead.'

'Of what?'

'An outbreak of plague, four days out of the Azores. I was unaffected, having survived a dance with the blue sickness myself, many years ago. I had to bury the last of my crewmates alone. Wrapped them in their own blankets, weighted them, and threw them in the sea. I'd thought at first I might handle the ship myself, return to São Miguel, but it was no use… a ship that size… And now I'll never see the islands…'

Ash and Garcia exchanged a look, both thinking precisely the same thing.

'Islands?' said Garcia. 'You mean Japan?'

Piero shook his head. 'No,' he said. 'The Fortunate Isles.'

Garcia scoffed. 'There's no such place.'

'Oh, there is,' said Piero, and reaching inside his robes produced a tattered scroll bound with red ribbon. He handed it to Ash, who removed the ribbon and unfurled the scroll to reveal an intricately drawn map.

'What is this?' she asked.

Piero eased himself up, resting on one elbow, and traced his finger across one side of the picture.

'Here,' he said, 'is the coast of Portugal. This is Africa, the Canary Islands. *These* are the Azores. And *here*, a thousand miles southwest of where we are now, lie the Fortunate Isles.'

'But no one has ever sailed that far,' said Garcia.

'Not true,' said Piero. 'A Genoese ship went that way eighteen months ago. They returned with *this map*, and with nuggets of gold as big as my fist. Diamonds the size of plovers' eggs. They said there was more treasure there than any ship could possibly carry. The *San Giorgio* was never sailing for China.'

V

Captain Lopez stomped from one side of his quarters to the other, his boots thudding heavily against the wooden floor. In brooding thought, he stroked his chin in the exact place where his beard was just beginning to grow back.

'And you believe him?' he asked.

Ash nodded.

Garcia seemed less certain. 'Gold nuggets the size of your fist? Diamonds the size of eggs?'

'Of *plovers'* eggs,' said Ash.

'He could be exaggerating,' said Garcia. 'You know how these things are.'

'But do we think it's worth pursuing?' asked Lopez.

Garcia shrugged. 'If what he says is true, then we – and His Majesty the King – will be rich beyond our wildest dreams. If, however, he is not, we could be sailing southwest for nothing.'

The Captain frowned. 'What was it St Jerome said, in his letter to the Ephesians?'

'You'll have to remind me.'

'Don't look a gift horse in the mouth.'

Marching past them, Lopez went up to the deck, Ash and Garcia following close behind.

'Listen up, men,' the Captain said. 'We're changing course, and sailing southwest. Our guest, the Genoese Piero, has given us a map. A map that will take us to the Fortunate Isles!'

A cheer went up across the deck, though Ash wondered if many of the crew knew what this meant. Before setting sail, they set fire to the *San Giorgio*, to consign its pestilence to the seabed, and by dusk the *Galgo* was heading towards an horizon the colour of freshly spilled blood.

VI

The first signs that they were near land were the gulls that greeted them one morning, cawing and howling over the deck, diving into the sea around the *Galgo* and emerging with wriggling fish caught in their beaks. An hour later, one of the crew spotted a single palm leaf floating by, as fresh and green as if it had only just fallen from the tree, and by noon Ash could see the first jagged outline of land, a single crooked outcrop followed quickly by the bumps and humps of other islands.

These islands, whatever they were truly called, were magnificent, each one towering into the sky and covered in vegetation, so that they looked every bit as emerald-encrusted as the stolen brooch in Ash's pocket. What's more, each one was fringed with a beach of pristine white sand.

The only obstacle between the *Galgo* and dry land was the pink coral reef that lay some distance from the shore. It would be impossible for the ship to get close without running aground, and so they would have to send out an expedition of smaller boats. But what did that matter? Piero of Lodi was right. There *were* islands here, and if he was right about the islands, then perhaps he was also right about the treasure.

It was finally agreed that ten of the *Galgo*'s crew would go to the largest of the islands. They waited overnight, the *Galgo* anchored a mile from the shore, and at first light lowered two small boats into the sea, and began their journey across the harbour.

In the first boat: Captain Lopez, Dr Garcia, Ash, Piero of Lodi and the single-eyebrowed boatswain named Fernando. In the second: the former lookout Diego, an apprentice pilot named Rodrigo, a carpenter named Oskar, another sailor named Bartolome and Pedro the steward. Side by side, the rowing boats crossed the harbour, the rowers struggling against a westerly current that moved around the largest island in a circle. Upon reaching the salt-white sand, the first thing that Ash noticed was the silence; an almost perfect stillness, but for the waves lapping gently against the shore. Twenty yards from the sand's edge began the dense, green jungle, but if anything was living in there, it didn't make a sound.

'Does that map of yours say *where* the treasure lies?' the Captain asked.

Piero shook his head. 'The men who returned said only that it lay *everywhere*.'

'Then we journey to the interior,' said the Captain.

No sooner had they entered the jungle, than the way became very steep, and they had to hack and slice a path through hanging vines and towering ferns. All around them stood enormous, gnarled old kapok trees, and in their branches birds as bright and colourful as tapestries, and timorous, large-eyed monkeys with furling tails and tapering, taloned hands.

They had been walking for quite some time when Ash spotted something at her feet; a curious, glistening ball that looked almost like ice, jagged and rough but crystal clear. She picked it up, finding it cool but not cold to the touch, and held it to the light. In seconds, she was surrounded by the others, all of them gazing in wonder at the mysterious rock.

'Is that…?'

'Can't be…'

'You mean…?'

Captain Lopez snatched it from her hand, studying it for himself. 'It's a diamond, all right,' he said.

'That's impossible,' said Garcia. 'Diamonds are mined out of the earth. They don't simply sprout up out of the ground like cabbages.'

'See for yourself,' said the Captain, passing him the stone. Garcia squinted at it for a moment, and his mouth fell open, as if he wished to speak, but had been rendered mute.

While all this was going on, three of their party had noticed something a little further ahead and one of them, Rodrigo, shouted, 'Captain! I think you should come and see this.'

Taking the diamond from Garcia and pocketing it for himself, the Captain led them on through the jungle to where Rodrigo, Fernando and Oskar were waiting anxiously, but it took a moment for them to see what all the excitement was about. The men stood on a small embankment, overlooking a shaded, shallow ditch.

'I don't get it,' said Ash. 'What am I looking at?'

In a low voice, Garcia replied, 'The gold. Look at all the gold.'

Sure enough, as Ash's eyes grew accustomed to the light, she saw that in the bottom of the ditch lay a stream of gold nuggets stretching as far, in both directions, as the eye could see.

All at once the others went running down the bank, like thirsty men towards a well, and began scooping up great handfuls of gold, laughing and cheering as they did.

VII

Night fell, and Lopez decided that rather than go back the way they had come and return to the *Galgo*, they would set up camp in the jungle and in the morning travel further into the island. Already they had filled several sacks with gold and various gemstones, leaving them on the path, to be picked up on their return journey. After all, it wasn't as if there was anyone around to steal them.

Ash wondered now if there was any point in taking that stolen lizard brooch to the Condottiero. What was two thousand ducats compared to just a fraction of what they'd found so far? She was so excited by the very thought of it, she could hardly sleep, and she knew the others felt much the same way. Only Garcia, Piero and the Captain seemed not to have let excitement overcome their common sense, and all three fell asleep almost as soon as they'd put out the camp fire; the Captain snoring loud enough to jangle the gold in his pockets.

Later, when their camp had been silent for some time, Ash heard some of the men, Rodrigo, Oskar and Diego, whispering among themselves.

'But how are we going to share it?'

'According to rank, the Captain says. After the King's share, that is.'

'Even them who's still on the boat?'

'That's what he says. Him getting the biggest cut, then first officer and so on.'

'But that ain't fair. Not if the others didn't come over. Why should any of them get a share? What we should do, lads, is go back telling the others we found nothing more precious than a coconut.'

'And keep it for ourselves, you mean.'

'Exactly my meaning.'

The Captain stirred, mumbling something in his sleep, and the three of them fell silent. Presently, they too were fast asleep, leaving Ash the only one awake. She stared up through the canopy of trees at a star-speckled sky, and wondered at the series of events that had brought her here; not just these last few weeks aboard the *Galgo*, but the years, decades and centuries since her childhood. Those very early days were not one but many lifetimes ago, and her memory of them felt more like half-forgotten dreams.

After so much time and so many travels, it seemed right that she should find herself on the edge of the world, but looking at the sky and at the stars she wanted more. She wanted what she knew was *up there.*

As, finally, she began to drift off, Ash thought she heard a sound from the distant hillside, a long and piercing wail that echoed out across the island. In her half-unconscious state, she couldn't tell if it was the howl of a wolf or a human scream.

VIII

Morning came, bringing with it a thunderstorm. No sooner had the first few drops begun to patter against the leaves than it became a riotous downpour, with raindrops as big as hazelnuts, and the ground around their camp turned instantly to mud.

Frantically, they gathered their things and took shelter beneath the largest nearby tree, waiting impatiently as the sky shook and flashed above them, until the rains began to die back down. Then they continued on their way, further into the jungle.

Ash wondered whether she should tell Garcia or the Captain about what she had overheard the night before. Maybe it was just innocent, idle chatter. Greedy men thinking greedily, without meaning a word they said. Or *maybe* that sort of talk could lead to mutiny, and if *that* were to happen, wouldn't she then shoulder some of the blame?

After climbing steadily uphill for what felt like hours they came upon a wide plain of tall grass, the ground damp and spongy beneath their feet. To the far side of the plain stood a mound which looked at first like a boulder of sandstone, but as the sky began to clear and the first rays of sun spilled down they saw it glitter almost blindingly.

'It looks as if it's *made* of gold,' said Garcia.

'I believe it is,' said Piero of Lodi. 'The Genoese explorers who came back from these islands said there were deposits of gold more massive than any seen in Europe or even Africa. It wouldn't surprise me if we were looking at one of them right now.'

With some difficulty, the men began to run across the plain, and that was when Ash heard it again, that strange and eerie howl she'd heard the night before.

'Did you hear that?' she asked.

'Hear what?' said Garcia.

'A howl, or something…'

Garcia stopped walking, and cocked his ear toward the sky. Then, within a second, it came again: that same mournful howl. The physician looked at Ash and nodded.

'I heard that,' he said. 'An animal of some sort. A monkey, perhaps?'

'Is that what they sound like?'

Garcia smiled softly. 'Wouldn't know,' he said. 'Can't say I've met that many of them. This is my first time out of Spain.'

They began walking again, picking up their pace to catch up with the others.

'Seriously?' asked Ash. 'You've never left Spain?'

Garcia shook his head. 'Never. How about you? I cannot place your accent. Where are you from?'

'Everywhere.'

'Elusive. No wonder you were a stowaway. Running away from something, or some*one*, I suppose?'

'That would be telling. How about you?'

The colour drained from Garcia's face, and Ash wondered if she had said the wrong thing. Then, just as suddenly as he'd paled, his expression brightened and he said, 'Seemed like a chance to see the world.'

Eventually, they reached the glistening mound at the far end of the plain and found, just as Piero suggested, that it was made entirely of gold.

'It can't be *real* gold, though,' said Rodrigo.

'I assure you, it can,' said Piero of Lodi. 'Our Genoese explorers described not one but countless deposits just like this.'

'Must be fool's gold,' said Diego.

Pushing his way past the others, Captain Lopez drew his dagger, and with a forceful slice he hacked away a sliver of the mound, which fell into the palm of his hand like a coiled spring.

'I've seen enough gold in my time to know the real thing,' he said, 'and this is gold.'

'But it must weigh *tons,*' said Oskar.

'We'll never get it back to the ship,' said Diego.

The Captain laughed. 'No we shall not,' he said. 'Some of the gold will just have to stay here.' He glanced around at his crew, studying their expressions, and smiled. 'Look at you all,' he said. 'Anyone would think there wasn't enough gold and precious stones just lying on the ground for each and every one of us to leave this island as wealthy as kings.' He wrapped the almost threadlike sliver around his thumb, twisting its ends to make a ring of it, and peered off into the distance. 'I think I see something,' he said, gesturing for Garcia to join him. 'There. Do you see? Looks almost like a…'

'… Temple,' said Garcia, as if he couldn't quite believe his own eyes.

Ash raised her hand to her brow and squinted. They were right. There, on the distant hillside, stood a flight of steps, three stone columns and the remnants of a pediment.

Lopez's one good eye flashed with an idea, and he beamed. 'You know what this place might be?'

Garcia shrugged.

'Gentlemen… and *lady*. I believe we may have found the Garden of Eden.'

Ash frowned and Garcia stifled a laugh. The others seemed less sceptical.

'Think about it,' said Lopez. 'An earthly paradise, far beyond the world…'

'But *Eden*?' said Garcia.

'Come,' said Lopez, already marching off across the plain. 'There's only one way for us to find out.'

The others began to follow, Ash and Garcia trailing behind by a few yards.

'This isn't Eden, though, is it?' said Ash.

'No it is not,' said Garcia. 'But that temple… It looks Greek, or perhaps Roman…'

'Our Genoese explorers described such structures,' said Piero, who had clearly been eavesdropping. 'They thought perhaps they were the remnants of a colony, founded by the Trojan diaspora. An acquaintance of Brutus or Aeneas…'

'I think,' said Garcia, 'that's even less likely than this being the Garden of Eden.'

They were halfway between the mound of gold and the temple when Ash heard another distant shriek or howl. This time the others heard it too, and they stopped in their tracks.

'What was that?' said Rodrigo.

'Local fauna of some kind,' said Lopez. 'A Barbary ape, perhaps. Nothing to worry about.'

'I've heard the Barbary apes of Gibraltar,' said Bartolome. 'And that didn't sound like no Barbary ape.'

'A jackal then,' said the Captain. 'Or some distant cousin of the wolf.'

Another howl rang out across the hills, echoing through the nearby valleys. Then another, and another, each coming from a different direction.

'I don't like this,' said Garcia.

'Me neither,' said Ash. 'Whatever's making that sound has us surrounded.'

Suddenly, something came whistling through the air towards them, zipping past Ash's ear, followed quickly by a wet thud, and Oskar the carpenter fell to the ground with an arrow in his back. Three more arrows followed, in quick succession, one burying itself in a tree, the other two finding their marks in Fernando and Pedro the Steward.

'Run for cover!' cried the Captain, and he led them into a dense thicket.

More and more arrows came after them, but none of them were hit. Then, turning on Piero of Lodi, Captain Lopez grabbed the Italian by his collar and began shaking him.

'You said nothing of tribesmen!' he growled. 'Did your Genoese explorers not think to mention that?'

Piero shook his head. 'They said the islands were uninhabited,' he whimpered. 'They said there were no people here.'

From the edge of the thicket, Ash gestured to the Captain and Garcia, beckoning them over.

'I don't think they're people,' she said, and joining her the two men followed her gaze and saw, up on the hillside, the archers who had fired on them; tall, muscular creatures with the bodies of men but the faces of fang-toothed wild dogs.

IX

'All right,' said Lopez. 'We don't have bows and arrows, so there's only one thing we can do, and that's split up.'

'Is that wise?' asked Garcia. 'Is there not greater safety in numbers?'

Ash shook her head. 'The Captain's right. They have the higher ground. We'd be like sitting ducks.'

Lopez smiled at her. 'We ought to start calling you Joan of Arc,' he said.

'Very well,' said Garcia. 'We split up. Then what?'

'We make our way to the beach, and row back to the *Galgo*,' said the Captain.

'But what about the gold and the jewels?' asked Rodrigo.

Lopez flashed him a scowl and shook his head. 'We pick up what we can along the way,' he said. 'But not so much that it slows us down. Whoever makes it to the beach waits no later than vespers, and if they find themselves faced with those… those *things*… they return to the *Galgo* regardless. Agreed?'

Everyone nodded.

'But what *are* they?' said Diego, who had been a greenish shade of white since the first onslaught.

All eyes turned on Piero of Lodi.

'I honestly don't know,' said the Italian. 'Our explorers didn't encounter them, so perhaps they are not of this island. The physician here is a man of science. Do *you* know what they are?'

Garcia shook his head. 'Perhaps some species undiscovered,' he said.

'Or men bewitched,' said Bartolome. 'Like the sailors turned to pigs by Circe.'

'It doesn't matter what they are,' said the Captain. 'What matters is that we make it off this island alive. Now. I'll take Piero, here. Dr Garcia, you go with Ash. Diego, Rodrigo, Bartolome… you three stay together.'

He gestured out towards the open plain.

'Piero and I will go left, into that gully. Garcia, Ash, you go back into the jungle. And you three… Follow that stream. Each way should take us back to the beach, but keep us covered.'

'Aye, Captain.'

'And as I said. Don't go slowing yourselves down with trinkets. Understood?'

'Aye, Captain.'

'Then let's go.'

Later, Ash would remember very little of how she and Garcia got back to the jungle. She would recall only the sounds of her feet squelching into the wet ground and her pulse, thundering in her ears. She remembered that her breath tasted coppery, like blood, from running so hard. She remembered looking across the plain and seeing, in the far distance, Bartolome cut down by an arrow to the chest. Everything else was a blur.

When, finally, she and Garcia were in the jungle they heard the canine creatures howling from the hillsides, and the last shower of arrows whistling through the air, thumping into the trunks of nearby trees or clattering to earth. Garcia collapsed onto his knees, breathless and shaking, and Ash saw tears forming in his eyes.

'We can't stay here,' she said. 'It isn't safe.'

She helped the physician to his feet, and together they walked deeper into the jungle. Ash had hoped they would find the path they'd made, that they would recognise some feature of their surroundings, but it wasn't to be. Every tree looked almost identical to the last, every bump or ditch had a twin or triplet every fifty yards, and when a fresh blanket of clouds passed across the sun it became impossible to tell which way was north or south.

They walked for several hours, but seemed no closer to the beach, and so decided to rest a while in a small clearing. It was some time since they'd last heard the monsters' howls. They might be safe here, for now. That said, they were running out of water. Ash's flask was empty, and Garcia's was down to its last drops.

As Ash rested with her back against a tree, Garcia went down on his knees and began muttering words she did not catch. When he was finished, she asked him, 'What were you saying?'

'I was asking God to deliver us from this place.' He stood, brushing the dirt and twigs from his knees, and took in a deep breath. 'But we should keep going,' he said. 'Or else we'll miss our boat.'

X

At first, they thought the dog-faced creatures had killed them, Diego and Rodrigo. The two men lay next to a stream, both dead, and it took a moment before Ash realised that they had, in fact, killed one another, each man still holding a bloodied dagger in his death-frozen hand.

'But why?' asked Garcia. 'When we have so many other enemies on this island, why turn on each other like that?'

Ash pointed to the ground around their bodies, which was scattered with nuggets of gold and uncut gemstones. 'Does that answer your question?'

'Greed, then,' said Garcia. 'The fools.'

What made it even more frustrating was that Diego and Rodrigo had chosen to have their duel within earshot of the beach. From where they now stood, Ash and Garcia could hear seagulls and waves brushing against the sand, and through the trees they saw a stark crescent of white against the sapphire sea.

But there was no time to bury the dead or mourn them. Already, the day was getting old, and the hour when Captain Lopez said any survivor should leave had long passed. Ash and Garcia ran the rest of the way, across the fringes of the jungle and down onto the beach, but though their ship was still anchored a mile out to sea, both of the rowing boats were gone, and the *Galgo* itself was too far away for them to signal anyone on board.

'They left us,' said Ash. 'I can't believe they just left us.'

'That doesn't make sense,' said Garcia. 'Why would the Captain and Piero take *two* boats? And why, if they've left, hasn't the *Galgo* set sail?'

Ash had to concede the physician was right, but it was getting dark, and though they'd filled their flasks at a freshwater stream, both of them were hungry. Together, they went back to the jungle, and began gathering wood to make a fire, and it was there Ash spotted a plump, fuzzy-feathered hen, pecking its way through the undergrowth. Realising it might make a satisfactory meal, she stalked after it as silently as she could, her dagger gripped between her teeth. Then, when the moment was right, she pounced.

Ash wasn't squeamish, she was more than prepared for the sight of blood, especially after the day they'd had. Having plunged her dagger into the hen, she was not, however, prepared for a shower of sparks and the smell of smoke.

Beneath the hen's feathers lay not flesh and blood, but cogs and coiled springs and strangely intricate panels attached to one another with brightly coloured veins. The creature's skeleton was made not of bone but metal. She returned to the beach, where Garcia had begun building their fire, holding the feathered automaton in both hands, and she dropped it to the ground next to the pile of wood.

'What *is* that?' asked Garcia, gazing down in horror at the exposed workings inside.

'It's a machine,' said Ash. 'I killed it, thinking we could have it for supper. But it's a *machine*.'

From the stacked firewood, Garcia took a piece of kindling and prodded at the hen, and all at once it came alive and began kicking its legs, the machinery inside whirring and ticking away like the workings of a clock. Then, just as suddenly as it had revived, it stopped.

'Do you think those creatures, the ones who attacked us, do you think *they* could have made something like this?' asked Ash.

Garcia shrugged. 'I don't know,' he said. 'I like to think myself a man of reason, but the things we have seen here… Truly, we are beyond the edges of the world…'

Then, from the jungle came a crackling sound, and in the fading light Ash saw two shadowy forms moving through the trees. She and Garcia bunched together, their backs against the sea. The only weapon they had between them was Ash's dagger, and it would be a poor match against a hundred arrows.

'Ahoy, there!'

The voice was instantly familiar: Captain Lopez, with Piero of Lodi following close behind.

As they came down onto the beach, the Captain said, 'So it wasn't *you* who took the boats?'

Garcia shook his head.

'Damnedest thing,' said Lopez. 'Must have been Diego and Rodrigo, the selfish swine.'

'It wasn't them,' said Ash. 'Both dead. Killed one another over the gold.'

'Then who took our boats?'

Piero of Lodi peered out to sea and scratched at his chin. 'Maybe,' he said, '*maybe* they were taken not by men, or by those savage beasts who attacked us, but by the sea.'

'Really?' said Garcia, raising an eyebrow.

'The currents,' said Piero. 'They move around the island in a clockwise motion. We felt it, as we were rowing across, did we not?'

Captain Lopez nodded.

'Then if the tide came in further than anticipated, taking our boats with it, the currents may have carried them to another part of the island.'

'Or further out to sea,' said Garcia.

'But as the tide recedes on this side, it will come in on the other,' said Piero.

Ash's face brightened. 'He's right,' she said. 'If we can get across the island, the boats may have washed ashore again.'

'And how will we get there?' said Garcia. 'The interior of the island is treacherous, and it's dark. We wouldn't last an hour in that jungle.'

'Perhaps,' said Piero. 'But what if we were to walk not over the island but *under* it? See for yourself.' He pointed across the bay, to a distant cove. 'There may be caves and tunnels that'll take us through to the other side.'

'Exactly,' said Garcia. '*May* be caves and tunnels. Alternatively, those caves and tunnels may lead nowhere.'

'And what is your plan, Doctor?' said Captain Lopez. 'That we wait here, on the beach, for our boats to wash ashore again. How long might that take? I say we try the caves.'

Garcia turned to Ash. 'What do you think?'

She thought for a moment. The idea of death, of danger, held little mystery or threat for her. She'd survived too many injuries that would have killed anyone else, lived through too many wars, massacres and plagues. There was nothing on this island that scared her quite as much as it should have, but the thought of spending an eternity here, watching these men die and living out her days entirely alone, was terrifying.

Now she looked at Piero, without whom they would never have come here. She could tell Garcia didn't trust him, that he still considered him a stranger. She had almost forgotten what those emotions were like. Getting to know someone, getting to trust them – it took days, weeks and months, sometimes even years, which must feel like an eternity to those whose lives come and go in decades. For Ash, a stranger was no less trustworthy than any other person. The time she had to judge them, to measure their character, seemed every bit as fleeting.

'I say we try the caves,' she said, and off they went, across the beach, each carrying a flaming torch, and leaving the remains of that strange mechanical bird far behind them.

XI

The light was fading fast, its final traces dying out in the west like embers but, around a low and rocky headland, they found the open mouth of a cave.

Crouching on his haunches, Piero of Lodi pointed into the darkness and said, 'Do you see?

There is a light at the far end. This should bring us out on the other side of the island.'

'That's assuming there is a beach,' said Garcia. 'And that our boats have washed ashore. And that we won't encounter any more of our dog-faced friends in there.'

'Shut your trap,' said Lopez. 'Right now, this is the best chance we have of getting off this island.'

Bracing themselves for the worst, the four of them entered the cave, and what struck Ash was how almost immediately they were engulfed by the dark. Living things crawled and scuttled about in the shadows, their clicking, clacking footsteps multiplied by echoes, and the torches were only bright enough to light the ground two or three yards ahead. Beneath their feet, the ground was rocky, uneven, and punctuated with shallow rock pools or slimy patches of seaweed.

Then, so suddenly it made the others – even Captain Lopez – jump, Piero of Lodi shouted, 'Look!'

He was pointing to the tunnel wall, but only as they gathered closer, the light of their torches coming together, could they see what he was pointing at. There, only a few yards away, fixed into the stone, was a door. Most curiously of all, it wasn't some mighty doorway carved from oak and studded with black metal, but a small grey rectangle, not much bigger than a man, with a plain silver handle to one side.

'I must be seeing things,' said Captain Lopez. 'Tell me, Garcia. Do I have my patch on the wrong eye?'

'You're not seeing things,' said the physician. 'That's a door.'

'But how is that even possible?' asked Ash.

Lopez went forward with cautious, tentative footsteps, as if approaching not a door handle but a venomous snake.

'Are you sure that's wise?' said Garcia.

Lopez glanced back at them, and for the first time Ash thought she saw in his expression not only trepidation but *fear*.

'Signor Piero?' he said.

'The choice is yours, Captain,' said Piero of Lodi. 'The choice *must* be yours.'

The Captain looked at Ash.

'And you, girl?' he said. 'What do you think?'

Ash nodded. 'Do it,' she replied, and Captain Lopez turned the handle.

XII

No sooner were they through the door than it slammed shut behind them, and they were wrestled to the ground by a band of assailants. Their torches fell, and in the dim and dying light Ash saw the faces of their attackers: the dog men from the plain, snarling and growling and gnashing their teeth. They were fiercely powerful, and had Ash, Garcia and even Captain Lopez pinned to the ground in a second. The only person they hadn't attacked was Piero of Lodi.

'What is the meaning of this?' roared Lopez, struggling and failing in the creatures' grasp.

'You remember the Caniforms?' said Piero, his voice different, his accent, his whole manner having changed in the time it took for him to cross the threshold. 'Human DNA spliced with that of a Rottweiler. Not that that'll mean much to you, of course. But it really is pointless putting up a fight, Captain. You'll only end up doing yourself a mischief. Now, I'll take these…' He grabbed first the Captain's dagger and then Ash's. 'And if you could just follow me.'

Not that they had much choice. Piero clicked his fingers, and the three of them were lifted off their feet and carried along by the creatures, the Caniforms, as if they were little more than marionettes. They were moving – or *being moved* – along a narrow passage, its walls flat, grey and featureless, and at the end of that corridor was a light so brilliant, after the darkness of the caves, that they could barely see what lay beyond.

From somewhere within the light they heard people cheering and clapping, like some carnival or festival, and music, loud and thunderous, but unlike any melody Ash had heard before. Then, emerging from the passageway they found themselves in the centre of a vast amphitheatre, like the arenas of ancient Rome, surrounded by hundreds upon hundreds of people; men, women and children dressed in curious clothes, waving banners and flags:

GO ASH!

CAPTAIN LOPEZ – OUR HERO!

WE ♥ GARCIA!

Above the crowds, six colossal screens flickered with bright colours and flashing images, words that neither Ash, nor Garcia, nor Lopez could possibly understand:

WELCOME TO BET-ZONE!

THE C-FISH FINESSE: LET'S CONNECTIFY.

FOR ICE-WHITE TEETH, CHOOSE DENTIFROST.

MCLINTOCK CANDY BURGERS! A BIG ROCK CANDY MOUNTAIN OF FUN!

The heart of the arena was a vast, circus-like ring, with three corridors leading off it, and in its centre three towering columns, each encircled by a spiral staircase.

'Ladies and gentlemen,' said Piero, his voice amplified and echoing. 'May I introduce our finalists: Francisco Lopez! Juan Luis Garcia! And Ash!'

The crowd began cheering and stamping their feet, so much so that the ground beneath them shook.

'I don't understand,' said Ash. 'What is this place?'

'This,' said Piero, his tone warm but patronising, 'is the Makaron, the largest in Bet-Zone's fleet of time ships.'

'Time… ships?' said Garcia.

'This is no ship!' said Lopez. 'It's an island!'

'The illusion is rather convincing,' said Piero. 'But no expense was spared in transforming the Makaron into a subtropical island. Though, I must say, young Ash here is the first person to try eating any of our animatronic wildlife.'

'And those creatures, the dog-faced men?' asked Ash.

'Genetically engineered plot twists!' said Piero. 'We tend to find they get things moving along.' Adding, under his breath: 'Plus, they make *great* merchandise. Action figures, stuffed toys… The kids love 'em.'

'But *why*? What's any of this for?'

'Let me show you!'

Piero pointed at the screens, and looking up Ash saw the events of the last few weeks played out for them, each moment seen from Piero's point of view: their discovery of the *San Giorgio*, their voyage to this island, their journey into the jungle…

'You see, the people here have been following your adventures very closely, haven't we, ladies and gentlemen?'

Another raucous cheer.

'We've given them exclusive odds on every choice you've made along the way. Will our intrepid heroes sail for the Fortunate Isles, or continue west? Which crew members will go to the island? Who will die in the first attack? Which ones will turn on one another? Right now, you are the stars of the galaxy's most popular intertemporal gambling experience!'

'Is that so?' growled Captain Lopez, though it was doubtful he'd understood a word Piero said. 'So what happens to us now?'

'Well,' said Piero. 'I'm very glad you asked.'

XIII

The three of them – Ash, Garcia and Captain Lopez – now stood on top of the three columns, twenty feet above the ground. In front of them was a kind of lectern, crafted of glass, with two buttons – one red, one green – in its slanted top.

When the cheering of the audience had died down, Piero explained everything:

'The game is simple. In a moment, each of you will press either one of those buttons. If all three of you press green, you're free to go. No questions asked. No further trials or tribulations. Your rowing boat awaits you, just outside this very theatre…'

To the far side of the arena, the iron gates in one of the passages swung open to reveal a flight of steps leading down to a beach and one of the two boats they had brought over from the *Galgo*.

'If one of you presses red,' he went on, 'they go through into the grand finale, and the chance to win a *million ducats'* worth of treasure…'

Another, even more deafening cheer from the audience.

'… Where they'll be joined by whoever pressed green first. The last player to press their button, or the only player to press green, will face instant elimination.'

'Elimination?' asked Ash.

'Courtesy of our friends at Artemis Lasers!' said Piero, pointing up to an array of cannon-like devices that were aimed directly at Ash, Garcia and Captain Lopez.

'However,' he continued, his tone now ominous, 'if all *three* of you press the red button, you will *die*.'

'This is monstrous!' shouted Garcia. 'You can't do this!'

'Oh, I think you'll find we can,' said Piero. 'And non-participation is *not* an option.'

From all sides of the arena, as if on cue, the Caniforms snarled at them, saliva dripping from their fangs.

Ash looked across at Garcia and Captain Lopez. The decision was simple. Three green buttons, and they were free. They'd leave without any treasure, but they'd escape with their lives. There wasn't any question of pressing the red button, was there? Not when if all of them did so, they would die.

Piero turned to the audience. 'You know what to do now, ladies and gentlemen. A million ducats is a *lot* of money in the world of 1485. Whoever presses the red button could walk out of here one of the wealthiest people on Earth. Will it be Ash, the young woman with a mysterious past? Or Dr Garcia, the enigmatic physician? Or how about Captain Lopez, the bellicose old seadog?'

'Who are you calling bellicose?' roared Captain Lopez. 'I'll have your guts for garters!'

Piero continued: 'Perhaps two or even three of them may have their eyes on those jewels, but if all three chase after the fortune, they will surely die! Which will it be? Ladies and gentlemen… Place! Your! Bets!'

Ash gestured to the others, to the Captain and Garcia, to get their attention.

'Listen,' she said. 'We have to all press green. It's the only thing that makes sense.'

Garcia nodded, but Captain Lopez remained almost expressionless.

'Captain?' said Ash. 'We could be *free*.'

But Captain Lopez said nothing.

'OK!' shouted Piero. 'The bets are now closed. It's time for our contestants to make their decision. They have thirty seconds… starting… now!'

On the six gigantic screens appeared identical clock faces, the narrow hand sweeping anticlockwise and counting down.

'Captain!' said Ash. 'Please. Think about this.'

Lopez closed his eyes, as if he thought it might stop her from seeing what he would do next. He took in a deep breath, let it out slowly, and in what Ash read as a gesture of remorse, he shook his head. Then he slammed his fist against the red button, and all around them the arena shook with the sound of cheering.

'No!' cried Ash. In that one move, the Captain had condemned at least one of them to death. But then a thought occurred to her, something she should have known from the start. What could they possibly do to harm her? What could their weapon, this 'laser', do to her that countless swords and knives and firearms had failed to do over the centuries?

'Dr Garcia!' she said. 'Press the red button.'

'I can't,' said the physician. 'If I do, they'll kill you.'

'It's all right. Trust me. I'll be all right. Look, if I press green, you *have* to press red, or you'll die.'

Garcia shook his head.

'Please. You *have* to.'

'I'm sorry, Ash. But I won't play their game.'

Angrily, Ash pressed her hand against the green button. Now Garcia had no choice. It was a case of pressing red, or certain death. But instead the physician simply smiled at her, and as casually as if he were pushing away an empty dinner plate, he pressed his hand on green.

'No!' said Ash, her voice drowned out by the crowds.

'We have a result!' shouted Piero. 'Captain Lopez chose red, which means he's automatically secured a place in the grand finale, while Ash and Dr Garcia both chose green, bringing it down to a question of who pressed their button first. And I can reveal that it… was… Ash!'

More cheering, more stamping of feet. Ash closed her eyes, fighting back tears.

'Sadly that means we have to say goodbye to one of our contestants. Dr Garcia. Have you had fun on board the Makaron?'

Garcia didn't speak, but Ash's eyes met his, and in those last few seconds something unsaid passed between them. Then, from high above came a deep and sinister hum, followed by an intense beam of red light that cut across the arena. In the time it took Ash to blink, the physician had vanished in a blizzard of black dust.

XIV

No sooner had the latest wave of cheering and stamping died down, than the Caniforms were on them again, shackling Ash and Captain Lopez and marching them down from the platforms. They led them across the arena and through the third corridor, into another vast, almost cathedral-like space.

In the centre of this room there stood what looked like a colossal iron cauldron, in the side of which was an opening. The Caniforms marched them forward, undid their restraints, and pushed Ash and Captain Lopez through the door, closing it behind them with a sonorous clang. They were alone.

'What is this place?' asked the Captain.

'How should I know?' snapped Ash. She glowered at him and shook her head. 'We'd be free now if it wasn't for you. And Garcia would be alive.'

'You think I came all this way to go home with *nothing*?' said Lopez.

Ash looked around, searching for a way out. To one side of the chamber, its end suspended an unreachable height above the ground, was a ladder, leading up to an aperture in the ceiling. To either side of the ladder were two circular metal handles, like ships' wheels.

'Welcome to the Grand Finale!' the voice of Piero came booming down from somewhere high above. 'If you look up, you'll see an outlet. In thirty seconds, water will start filling the tank. It takes the average human one hundred and fifteen seconds to climb the ladder, but only ninety seconds for the tank to fill with water. Each of those two valves will stop the flow in two minutes, but if both are turned at the same time, they will turn the water off in one.'

'Mathematics,' growled Captain Lopez. 'I *hate* mathematics.'

'No,' said Ash. 'This is more than that.'

'Your time,' said Piero. 'Begins now!'

The metal ladder dropped down to their level with a sudden clang, and ice-cold water began cascading from the outlet above, splashing around them first in puddles, then rising up around their feet and then their ankles. Ash ran across the tank, and began turning one of the wheels.

'We have to stop the water,' she said. 'Come on. Help me.'

Captain Lopez looked up at the aperture and then the ladder.

'Hundred and fifteen seconds for the average human,' he said. 'I reckon I can make it in less.'

'No!' said Ash. 'If we work *together*, we can cut the water off in a minute.'

'Rather you than me,' said the Captain, and hoisting himself up out of the rising water he began climbing the ladder.

For a moment, Ash paused. She could join him, climb up after him. They'd both drown, of course, but for her it would last only a moment before she'd revive. She *could* do that. After all, the Captain had doomed poor Garcia. They would be free now, if it wasn't for him. But no. She couldn't bring herself to do that, and so instead, she carried on turning the valve, working until her arms ached, and the water was above her chin, and then her lips, and then her nose...

Ash kept going for as long as she could, turning and turning the wheel, but eventually she could hold her breath no longer. Against every instinct in every fibre of her being, she breathed in, felt the bitter chill of water flooding into her lungs, and seconds later her world went silent and dark.

XV

When eventually she came round, Ash found herself back in the arena, coughing up gouts of cold water, and as her eyes began to focus she saw Piero standing over her with an expression of disbelief.

'That's... impossible...' he said.

She sat upright, and the audience gasped, as if they were witnessing a miracle: the girl who only moments ago had drowned, right up there on those giant screens, back from the dead. Her clothes and hair were drenched, and she was freezing. Next to her, lying on his back, was Captain Lopez, the ground around him wet, his eyes closed and his skin as white as marble. There'd be no miracles for him.

'Tell me,' said Ash, getting to her feet. 'How many of your "players" ever make it out of there?'

Piero backed away from her nervously, as if he were looking at a ghost, which – to all intents and purposes – he was.

'N-n-none,' he stuttered. 'One person always chooses to think only of themselves. And we've never had three players press green.'

'Thought so.'

'But you... you *drowned*.'

Ash shook her head. 'I breathed in water and I passed out,' she said. 'But I never drown. Trust me. This wasn't a first.'

She looked up at the audience, casting her gaze across their shocked and slack-jawed faces. What kind of people were they?

'So what happens now?' she said. 'Have I won?'

'I... I don't know,' said Piero. 'We've never had a winner. And the laws are very clear.'

'Which laws?'

'Governing time travel. We're not allowed to leave behind any evidence we were ever here.'

'I see.'

'But you've seen us… you know what we are…'

Piero gestured to the Caniforms, who were standing guard on every exit, and they began making their way forward, forming an ever-tightening circle around them.

'I'm sorry,' said Piero. 'You really were a very popular contestant, but we can't let you go.'

'Oh, really?' said Ash, and reaching into her pocket she produced the gem-encrusted brooch she'd stolen in Seville. Then she leapt at Piero, grabbing him by the hair and placing the lizard's sharpened tail against his throat. 'Make one move, and you'll regret it,' she said. 'Now tell your dogs to back off.'

'I… I can't do that…'

'Do it, or you'll die.'

Piero nodded, and with his voice quaking in fear said, 'Step down. *Step. Down.*'

One by one, the Caniforms backed off, looking at one another as if wondering what to do next. They snarled and growled, but didn't make a move.

With Piero still in a chokehold, Ash edged her way across the arena, towards the corridor that led down to the beach. For the first time in what felt like aeons she heard the world outside; the wind rustling through the trees, the sea crashing against the shore, and down the corridor they went, Piero trembling in her grasp. Behind them, at the far end of the corridor and silhouetted by the lights, Ash saw the Caniforms massing together.

'Tell them to stay right where they are!' she hissed in Piero's ear.

'Stay back!' said Piero. 'Don't come any further!'

Once they were outside, Ash saw that they were on the far side of the island, on an unfamiliar beach lit only by starlight. There, nestled in the sand only a short distance away, was one of their two rowing boats, and Ash made Piero push it down to the water, giving its hull an occasional kick herself to speed up their progress.

All across the hillside, above the arena's entrance, stood more of the Caniforms, the same archers who had attacked them on the plain. They watched them in silence, their expressions blank and pitiless, and did nothing as Ash and Piero clambered into the boat. Then, the brooch still firm against his throat, Ash ordered Piero to start rowing.

XVI

On the deck of the *Galgo*, surrounded by men armed with muskets and cutlasses, Piero confessed all. He and the people inside the island came here from a world fifteen centuries in the future. Though they found it hard to believe, the crew understood the concept of a wager. To Piero and his audience, this world in their distant past was sport; the crew of the *Galgo* and – before them – the *San Giorgio*, were just names who had been lost at sea.

'We've done it so many times,' Piero said, sobbing as he spoke. 'Roanoke, HMS *Blenheim*… These names won't mean anything to you, I suppose…'

Then, his tale told, he begged for mercy.

'Mercy?' said Ash. 'You ask *me* for mercy? After you killed all of the others. After you turned us against each other. Made a sport of us. You ask me for mercy?'

Timidly, he nodded.

This was it. The balance of life was now in her hands, not his. The desire to have the men shoot him where he knelt was overwhelming. If these last few days – indeed, her entire *life* – had taught her anything, it was that people look out only for themselves; that greed will always win, even when it means losing everything.

'Please,' said Piero. 'Let me go. We'll leave, I promise you. We'll leave and never come back.'

The men looked to Ash for their cue. Could she do it? Could she give the nod and have them kill this pathetic, unarmed man in cold blood? What if humanity is only so bad because, when it comes to a question like this, so many make the wrong decision?

Moments later, Piero was in the rowing boat, alone, and making his way back to the island. The rest of the *Galgo*'s crew seemed more surprised than impressed by Ash's clemency, but they didn't know what she or any of the others had been through.

It took Piero an age to reach the shore, but the crew of the *Galgo* watched him the whole way. Below decks, the gunners manned the cannons, prepared for any attack these people from the future might make, but none came.

Moments after Piero had run back into the mountain, something incredible happened. The current that moved clockwise around the largest island stopped in a tumult of surf, and the sea began to bubble and boil. As if experiencing an earthquake, the islands rumbled and shook, and from somewhere deep inside the mountains came a drone that grew louder and louder. From beneath the sea there came a blazing light that rose up out of the water and surrounded the islands in a vast and shimmering globe. Then, with a sound like thunder, they were gone, and the waves rushed in to fill the void they'd left behind.

In the moments that followed, the *Galgo* was tossed about in its wake, its hull creaking and groaning against the churning waves, its sails flapping noisily against the wind, but it stayed afloat. Then there was calm, and all about them lay nothing but the ink-black sea.

XVII

The *Galgo* returned to Seville some six weeks later, having lost only nine of its crew. Though some of its men gave second-hand accounts of savage, dog-faced creatures and an archipelago that vanished, an age of wisdom and enlightenment soon turned those stories into folktales and myths. Seven years after that fateful voyage, a Genoese captain named Columbus discovered a continent another thousand miles beyond the islands the *Galgo*'s crew described. As for Ash, she too vanished into legend, and no woman of that name was ever heard of again.

If, however, you happen to visit the Uffizi Gallery in Florence, you may be interested to note that a certain portrait, depicting the reputed mistress of a famous Condottiero, shows a very beautiful woman wearing a lizard-shaped brooch, with emeralds for scales and rubies for eyes.

The Triple Knife

Jenny T. Colgan

AUGUST 9TH 1348

And now I will write in English even though it is a language that sticks in my troat. Trout. Throat. *Alors*. So. *Donc*.

A new journal for a new journey, as there is nothing to do now except watch the rocking of the bow and listen to Essie's astonishment – my little French *enfant* – at what these English consider acceptable to serve for *dîner*.

I sang for Johann:

'Rough blows the North Wind… cruel blows the East…
heavy blows the South Wind… we all fall BENEATH!'

and he giggled as I tickled him under the arm, and Rue laughed because he always laughs when Johann laughs, and also he is simply one of those babies who likes to be happy; but Essie wasn't distracted at all, even as the boat pitched and rolled and we clung on to the rough wooden bench so hard I took a splinter.

Instead she looked up, away from the food, with that look on her thin face and glint in her dark eyes that I recognised immediately, and I realised I was in for an 8-year-old's inquisition, which is as relentless as a witch hunt, and I know a bit about those.

'*Maman*?'

'Mm?'

'Why did we leave Marseille again?'

'In English, please.'

She sighed crossly and repeated the question in that clunky, phlegm-ridden tongue I have painstakingly been teaching them all.

'Well, I told you. We are going to the greatest city in the world! The largest city since Rome! For adventures.'

Essie pouted. 'And why isn't Papa coming?'

'Because Papa is going to look after the fishing nets all safely for us until we have had enough adventures, and then I will send you home,' I said, because it was true.

I had… what is the good English phrase, there, I know it: I had sworn *blind*, never again, but… oh, but Tomas had been. Well.

So handsome I never saw, and he such a quiet man, practically silent. Never asked a question. Never fussed me. No curiosity about why I had a crown in my locked chest, or why, if he or I woke for any reason in the night my sword would be in my hand and at his throat before you could say, 'It was just the thunder, Alys, get back to sleep.'

As for the babies coming, the stupidity was all mine, and then there was Essie, and suddenly, from the second those tiny ageless eyes opened on my breast, sweetness and happiness was mine too, for the first time: a surprise, as I had always considered babies simply an irritating burden, like ringworm, or immortality, or frostbite.

And so I told myself Johann and Rue were essential really; so they could protect and comfort each other when I had to leave them. As, one day I will. As I have to leave everyone as they turn curious, then suspicious, then horrified, then superstitious and finally murderous, and I think, well, my own children could not do that, but I have seen children do things to parents too, terrible things, because I have seen everything, and I know I could not bear it.

And so we are leaving Tomas, so that even my quiet man cannot say one more time, it's astonishing, truly, is it not strange that three babies and twenty years have not marked you, no, not an inch, and does your hair not grow?

August 10th

The bark creaked. I paid a lot of gold for this tide. Thank goodness it turned early, before Tomas had even stirred. Essie disappeared, and I found her behind a heaped chest of shining oranges, bent over in concentration.

'What are you doing now?'

I have no fear of the other sailors as a woman alone: they are good enough men on the whole, and I made a point of standing on the prow first day and juggling knives. I pretended it was to entertain the littles, but when I threw them under the boson's legs and caught them without looking, glinting in the sun, I believe they got the message more or less.

'Ugh,' said Essie. 'They served pig gruel for breakfast.'

'The food is different in Britain to France.'

'You should tell them,' she said. 'Pig food is for pigs and please may we have some human food please thank you very much also tea.'

She is obsessed with this new idea of tea. I smiled as the greasy-faced boy who acts as 'cook', if you could call it that, overheard this and grimaced and I distracted her quickly.

'I liked it,' said Johann quietly, hiding behind my skirts. It's true, he likes everything, and I caressed his curly head.

'Well, you shall make a fine strong English lad,' I said and he smiled and stuck his tongue out at his sister.

'Look, *Maman*!' said Essie, ignoring her little brother.

It was then I noticed the rat in the dim corner, bigger than a kitten. He was an ugly brute, but I was pleased to see him. When you can't find a rat: that's the time to worry about a ship.

'Don't touch him,' I said. 'He might bite you.'

She showed me a small piece she must have prised off the wheel of good Nederlander cheese I brought wrapped in a cloth.

'He likes this.'

'I expect he does. He likes fingers too.'

'You won't eat me, will you Rose?' said Essie, leaning towards the rat, who hissed.

'Rose?'

'It's a pretty name.'

I looked at her. 'I suppose it is. But don't let it get too close.'

It was too late. The rat was already nibbling from her fingers because, one, Essie disobeys everything I ask her to do as a matter of principle, and two, she loves all creatures, animals, the weaker and the younger the better. She always has. I know I should teach her to stay away from the weak; to seek out the strong and close her ears to everyone else. I've seen it time and time again; it's the only way not to stumble by the wayside. But it doesn't matter; I can't change her. And in truth I don't want to. She is the very, very best of me.

'There you are, Rose! Nice and delicious, yum yum yum!'

I realised Essie was now giving her lunch to her rat. He didn't seem to like it much either.

I glanced over to where a couple of the sailors were tossing Rue in the air to make him giggle. He's become quite the pet. Johann was watching enviously, and so I went over and grabbed him impulsively, clambered up the steps out of the musty below decks and onto the foredeck, where the spray was lighting the air, so fresh and salty it made you gasp, and the little bark was tossing down and up, but none of us gets sick easily; and instead I swung Johann round and round as he giggled and his little hands grabbed my shoulders and I twirled him into the netting, just as someone shouted, 'Land ahoy!'

I stopped whirling Johann, who shouted, 'More, more!' and instead stopped and smelled the cool earth as we glided into the deep mouth of a river; someone said 'South of Hamp Town', and people on the wide, wide beaches stopped from what they were doing – gathering eels in their nets, the midshipman told me – and looked up. There were cooking fires dotted across the bone-white sand, and they looked like tiny stars.

August 13th

'Why is it so big, *Maman*? Who are all these people? They are dressed strangely.'

'You have a lot of opinions for an 8-year-old.'

'In Marseille, they have silk,' Essie had returned serenely, as we finally reached our lodgings, beating off the clamouring hands of the young grubby boys who had accosted us at every town shouting, 'Lodgings? Safe! Clean! Carry your bags,' despite the fact you could see the lice dance on them even as they spoke.

'And also it is almost mostly definitely not raining at home,' said Essie.

'Look up,' I said.

The houses fell against each other like weary travellers – many timbered, two-storeyed, collapsed drunks, shop signs creaking in the breeze. And above them were the great stained-glass windows of the cathedral, their colours holding an exhausted Johann in its spell. Also, the longer they looked up at the great church, the less time they spent looking at the iron poles with the remains of traitors on them, and the crows that perched there.

I have been to Trondheim, and to Paris, so I consider myself knowing in the ways of cities, but this place is different altogether; so vast, so filled with different people, so empty of anyone who would give us a second glance amongst the rowdy jugglers, the shouting sellers, the mendicants, the soldiers and the priests, of course. Always the priests.

I kept all our clothes plain to avoid notice as we pushed through the throng, but I had enough gold sewn into the lining of my cloak to find us decent lodgings near the Moor's Gate, far enough away I thought from the stench of the tanneries, but I was wrong about that.

Essie was quiet and tired after the long journey, and I felt nauseous myself. We were long enough in the cart, next to a French woman, Madame Bellice, who kept her nose buried in a bouquet of lavender that reminded me of Provence, and protested that the English stank of old milk. Johann burbled to her in French but she was indefatigably uncharmed, then Essie started being rude about her in English and required a scolding I did not truly mean and kept smirking through.

It served me right when I turned up to our new lodgings and found she was lodged just across the street. I don't care. I don't make friends.

The road bustled full of people making their way to or from the smarter merchant's homes, leading donkeys laden with meat, fish I could already tell would not be welcome, spices I had not smelled in years and bolts of cloth, all colours. I had to tug Johann away from the spectacle that was simply daily city life.

We entered our new home, which had straw, clean enough, on the ground; a clear fireplace and a bed for us all and a cot for the baby. I have seen rather worse.

Essie was looking pale and white, and I grabbed a pot from my bag just in time as she threw up into it.

'I'm not sure you're the best traveller,' I said, then I got distracted by something squirming under her sack.

'You didn't bring Rose?'

She looked up at me, her brown eyes absolutely huge in her heart-shaped face. 'She's my friend, *Maman*,' she said. 'I'm sure she didn't like living on that boat.'

The rat regarded me malevolently.

'I'm sure she didn't,' I said. 'But there are enough rats in this town already.'

'Please can we keep her?' Essie's eyes were rimmed with pink. The rat was biting furiously at the handkerchief she'd tied him in.

'Darling, get some rest,' I said. 'We'll see in the morning.'

'That means no!' said Essie, in that confused fury of extremely fatigued children. '"We'll see" always means "No"!'

'Get some rest,' I said shortly. Rue didn't look well either. And of course that rat will be long gone in the morning, hopefully a poor man's breakfast.

I stepped outside to dispose of Rose, who suffered at the end of my sword a cleaner death than most of my enemies.

At the corner of our lane, I heard a commotion and moved closer to the wall. It is my new aim: to avoid confrontation. I've seen enough of fighting, I think. Surely. For now.

To my surprise it was Madame Bellice, the lady from the carriage and now our neighbour. She was screaming and yelling, and a thick crowd had of course gathered round, but nobody would go near her.

'Look at me!' she was screaming. 'Find me a physician.'

I glanced through the crowd. She was holding up her hands and screaming in pain. Large black growths were visible underneath her arms. The women in the crowd were running away with their children. Suddenly she saw me.

'Madame! Madame! Alys! *Aidez-moi!* Help me!' she cried, sweat running off her, her eyes completely wide in terror.

'I have children,' I said, but her face was so desperate I approached, telling Johann, who trots everywhere after me like a puppy, to stay back.

'I am so sick,' she said. 'Please, please, find me a physician, a doctor.'

'Is there a doctor?' I said to the crowd, but nobody turned round or identified themselves.

'It's the plague!' shouted one man suddenly and the crowd gasped. I heard rumours of plague too, coming up from the Nubians, but had not seen it. Surely it was not here.

'She's got the plague! God have mercy on us!'

A cold hand clutched my heart. She was in our carriage. Or, we were in hers.

Instantly the people dispersed, running, some of them. It was fun, apparently, watching the crazy lady, but the diseased lady, that's a little too much.

I hissed at Johann to stay by our doorway on the other side of the street. I was about to leave when I heard a heartrending sob come from Madame Bellice.

Ach. Motherhood has ripped a layer of skin right off me. She was sobbing exactly like Johann did when Essie broke his wooden dog by washing it in the river; as if the world would end.

I sighed. I already knew not much can harm me.

I led her inside her lodgings, which were much like ours, and laid her down. Her room was heavy with sweat, waste and disease. I looked around for clean straw for her bed, but there was none, so I laid the least dirty rug down instead.

'Lie down and I'll go to the well for you,' I said in French. 'You have to boil the water.' I learned this trick on the silk route, from a Japanese woman almost older than I am, and it has not failed me yet.

'It hurts so much,' she said, wild eyed and thrashing. 'Make it stop! Make it stop!'

'I'll try and find someone to help,' I said, looking around, although this woman had the stink of death on her, and once it begins, it is a timely fool's errand to try and reverse it.

I turned to leave to fetch the water, but suddenly there was a shadow cast through the sun of morning; an ominous shape appeared in the doorway. It startled me.

It was a man, but wearing a strange mask, like the huge beak of a bird, in some sort of leather. He also wore a broad hat fanning out from his head, and a long cloak, all in the same material. He reminded me of the crows I had seen at Traitor's Gate.

I stepped forward. 'Yes?'

'I am a Scientist,' stated the figure in a strange, accent-less voice. I had not heard this word before. I stepped back.

'Are you the physician? Can you help?'

'I will examine. It will help.'

'No,' said the Madame, suddenly terrified and shrinking away from him. And it was true: the man had a sinister countenance.

'This is the doctor come. He can help you,' I said, although I was not sure about either of these things.

The figure came forward, opening a black bag he had with him. He had a strange gait. 'Let me examine you.'

Suddenly outside I could hear Essie screaming '*Maman! Maman!* I'm sick again!' I froze as icy water cascaded through my heart.

'I have to go,' I said.

The figure continued to approach. Something struck me as strange about him, but I couldn't tell what it was, and was too torn to care.

'Don't leave me,' begged the woman in a guttural tone. 'Don't leave me.'

Outside Essie shouted my name once more.

'I have to,' I said and backed away. 'Good luck. Look after her,' I commanded the medicine man, who opened his big black bag full of instruments, like a dentist, or a surgeon or a butcher, and did not respond.

And I left and ran to Essie and picked her up in my arms and took her home, just as Madame Bellice began to scream.

AUGUST 15TH

AUGUST 16TH

Oh, the fevered days and endless nights, no better for knowing I cannot be relinquished, for I would have willingly been relinquished.

August 17th

August 18th

The soldiers came this morning. But it was my least bad night: the buboes were shrinking, the children slept, finally, wiped out, but sleeping, and I thought, 'We are through; we are finally through this.'

I had made us drink lots of water boiled over the fire, trying to force the sickness from our bodies and finally this morning, although I was exhausted, I was almost better and could stand. The children seemed better too, and I was heating up some oats for our breakfast and wondering if all the bread in London was mealy and black or if the town warranted more investigation, when I heard a pike at the door. I recognised it immediately.

'Open up!' called the soldier.

I rolled my eyes. I thought we had been through enough in London town. 'Yes, yes, right away, just coming,' I shouted back cheerily.

I hushed the children and quickly took out my knife. Whatever they required, if there's one thing I've learned about soldiers it's this: getting captured is the first mistake. I am not the spoils of war.

Always move first. If he thinks he's listening for a woman who'll be cowering back protecting her children, then he'll have another think coming.

'Open…'

I hurled the door open with my foot and whacked my knife up against the side of his neck, holding it there before he had a chance to notice what had happened, and kicked the pike out of his hand. It clattered onto the muddy street.

'What do you want?'

'Unhand me.'

His fellow came round from the other side. 'Put the knife down!' he commanded.

He expected me to turn my face in his direction and answer him. So I did not do this; instead, I darted out quick as a snake and tripped him in the mud, ramming my foot somewhere I knew it would hurt.

'NOW!' I shouted. 'ANSWER ME!'

So. It turns out England is not in the least like the Hundred Years War, and they have all these rule of law things and everything.

I was locked up in a white tower, with a broken toe and the usual cuts and bruises, which didn't bother me in the slightest, even though one of the gaolers looked slightly shamefaced at locking up a lady;

whereupon he tried to handle the tile around my neck and I shoved him away.

So I am locked up fairly comprehensively, even by my standards (I have checked for the usual: wall coverings for ladders; bars I can squeeze through; persuadable guards, so far without joy. They didn't look even tempted. Perhaps everything I have heard about English men is true).

A rather charming *gentilhomme* called Godfroi came to interview me; he had the nose of a hawk, and a profile that could only be English; his neck sloping straight down from the chin; a soft voice that did not need to shout to bring authority, for who in England does not know their estate?

They tied me to a chair in a windowless torture dungeon with a fire roaring, although it is summer time, and an array of pokers and pliers to scare me, which cheered me mightily as both make excellent weapons, and they had left me with none.

The man coughed. 'So you are newly arrived, and you are accused of spreading the sickness.'

'Why would I move to a country and try to kill everybody in it?'

The man shrugged. 'In my experience that is precisely what foreigners do.'

I folded my arms. 'Well, it's not true. I've had it myself.'

The man coughed again. At first I thought he simply had the pallid flesh of his countrymen. Now I realised he himself was pale and sickening, fast.

'Half your street is dead. And it is carrying on. But you, we see, are not dead. Did you do this by witchcraft? Can you stop it?'

'Is this a trial? I have my own ducking stool.'

'Bringing sickness is punishable by death,' he said, coughing again.

I glanced at the instruments by the fire. He saw me looking and beckoned over his guards to stand closer. Two guards. I turned my gaze away in case he saw in my eyes that two dozen might just about give us a fair fight.

On the other hand there was a moat to swim and locks to navigate and I was very tired and anxious to get home to my littles.

'There are physicians,' I said suddenly. 'There was a doctor on the street.'

He looked up. 'What kind of a doctor?'

'They say they do science. They can fix things.'

'Where were they from?'

'I couldn't tell. They were wearing masks.'

'Fools and tricksters,' he said. 'Preying on the sick and the stupid.'

'Maybe,' I said.

He looked at me, his pale eyes curious. And something else. Desperate.

They left me in the torture chamber for a long time. Certainly long enough to loosen my bonds. So much for the most feared prison in England. I once spent a season getting tied up every night by a young monk in a flagellant's monastery in Amiens. We both learned a lot that year.

'Essie knows how to get to the well,' I thought. 'Please, please, please, let her remember to boil the water.'

Godfroi returned as I heard guards tramping back in, cross and empty-handed. They had found no strange physicians; just legions and legions of the dead or nearly dead.

I realised then I simply had to leave. My three chicks needed me.

'Sorry…' I leaned over as Godfroi entered. 'I shouted but nobody would respond… but I remembered one other thing they said about where they were going to be… I'm so, so sorry not to have mentioned it before…' My tone was conversational and light and I leaned forward to talk in a conciliatory manner with the visibly weakening interrogator. 'I think they said they were going to be in—'

I kicked out my chair and brought up my knee, which made the table ricochet off his bent-forwards forehead, practically knocking him out.

The guards jumped towards me but I grabbed a poker and a set of tongs in either hand and, bang, threw my arms up on either side like I wished to fly. They both went reeling and I grabbed Godfroi, removed his knife, and hauled him towards the door. He looked almost relieved someone was propping him up; he weighed almost nothing. Not only that, but he didn't pull away or resist me in any way. I gave him an enquiring glance.

'If I'm your prisoner,' he said weakly, 'will you take me to see these doctors?'

'Yes,' I said grimly.

'Let her pass,' he whispered hoarsely to the other guards who were gathering on the stairs. 'I am her hostage and her powers are legion. Let us pass I command you.'

We burst down the stairs and onto the bright street, and I hailed a boatman to take us up river. He took us without commenting on the knife I held, although he did mew that he could not go further than Aldgate at this time of day and I said, 'You will,' and used Godfroi's sword to rip open the hem of my coat, and scattered the gold within on the prow.

*

The street was quiet, and I tore towards my door, the man in tow.

'*Maman!*' came a voice and I nearly screeched in relief and joy and pulled Essie, pale, so thin, into my arms and whirled her around.

'I took good care of Rue,' she whispered, and I wiped his precious brow and hoisted him onto the sling on my back, which had felt so empty, and Johann clung to me with filthy dirty fingers and my heart burst with joy, and I gave gold to Essie and told her to go to the bakers and buy every sweetmeat they had.

'Set me down,' said Godfroi. I had forgotten all about him; he was leaning against a wall, breathing heavily; he could have run away a hundred times and I would not have cared a whit, but here he was, panting, diminished so.

I let him lie on my good rug, which shows I am not evil in fact. Johann padded over and patted the man on his strange pale hair and looked up at me questioningly.

'Is he our new friend?'

'Hmm,' I said.

Essie came slowly back from the bakers with a few tired cakes in her basket. 'No more cakes,' she said sadly. 'The lady said no more cakes, for the baker is dead.'

I looked for the cheerful words I could put on this and found none, except that, like me, thank goodness the children appeared to be over the sickness and thus immune, like their measles and their quinsy. So I put out the stale honey cakes anyway.

'These taste old, *Maman*,' complained the little gourmande, after one bite.

'I like them,' said Johann, looking at me hopefully for praise. I let the baby suck on one; let his gummy paws sticky as a cub in honey whilst I tended to Godfroi on the floor, grateful that my children were past the danger.

'Water?'

But he couldn't keep a thing down and I turned my head as I felt, rather than saw, the shadow at the door.

This time there were three of them, all the same size and shape, with those great pointed beaks on their faces.

They moved smoothly and slowly and I realised what it was that was so strange about them: they did not smell as we did.

They did not smell of England or of the North or of France or everywhere I had been on Earth: of blood; old straw, of livestock, of the latrines we trod through every day in rivulets on the streets; of the old food and fetid cheese and turned meat we ate in town, or the curds of country living; the special smell of gaps of teeth in the mouth, the ancient salty sweat from clothing never removed and cuts undressed: the proper, natural rich and loamy deep smell of all the things that live.

They smelled of a place I had been once before, a long time ago; a clean, empty space without muck or soil. Oh yes. I had smelled it before.

A spaceship.

I could scarce remember the word. But oh, my body remembered, for my eyes started blinking rapidly, and my heart pounded, and I felt a feeling of battle soak through my veins.

These men... they came from those places beyond the stars. I looked at their masks again. I did not see straps, or joins. Were they even masks at all?

I stepped forward. But were they friends, like the girl in the box? Or false friends, like the man in the box? Or destroyers, like Odin?

And if they were friends... My heart leapt again. No more trying to scratch a living day by day. We could go, out into that wild universe where creatures such as me were not unknown; where there were lives we could have where I did not lie; where I did not have to give up my children and pretend to be unknown to them; where I was not unnatural; where I did not have to lie and kill and cheat every day of my life simply to get by.

I stepped forward. 'Here they are,' I said to Godfroi, whose pallid face had taken on a hopeful look as they entered.

Johann stood behind me. 'Scared, *Maman*! Bad men!'

'Not to you,' I whispered carefully, keeping my eyes on them.

The Scientists took out a sharp implement with something I had not seen for a long, long time: a light that was not fire.

Once again, excitement lit up my breast. Johann forgot his shyness and came out to gaze upon the tool in wonder. Essie looked at me, happy and excited like she was at a travelling fayre. The instrument gave out a beam of violet light that crossed the room.

Oh yes. I had seen lights like that before. Lights from other worlds, other places.

'Don't touch it,' I said, feeling Rue's grabby fingers behind me. 'Don't!'

I hastily unbundled Rue and shoved him into Essie's arms. I had to see what was happening, but they did not.

'All of you. Outside,' I said. 'Outside, now'

Essie opened her mouth to protest, but for once she listened to me. It was Johann who was transfixed by the lights and I had to push him sharply through the open doorway, although it pained me to do so. 'Go!'

There was a hissing noise as the beam of light started to travel across the floor.

'You see,' I said boldly to the Scientists, 'I have a proposition for you. For where you came from…'

I had no idea what my proposition actually was, but I felt we had to start somewhere. All three ignored me, however, their beaks following the path of the light, and the man on the floor.

'Help me!' moaned Godfroi in supplication.

And then, in an instant, all was whited out in a scream as the travelling light entered his shoulder and carried on, until the arm fell, with a thump, clean off on the floor and then even the scream was cut off, as he quickly dropped into a merciful faint as the light somehow stopped the wound from bleeding – I could not tell why nor how.

'What are you?' I said, rushing to Godfroi's side, even as one of the figures picked up the discarded arm and started examining the black lumps on it. He cut through the arm quickly and efficiently, as the other man came up with strange black bags that, I now realised, buzzed and moved as they were filled.

'What are you? What are you doing?' I said.

One glanced at me. 'We are Scientists,' he said.

'You said that. I don't know what the word means.'

'We discover things. We test things. We work on things that are harmful and make cures.'

'Are you going to cure the plague?'

The masked man nodded his head. 'Yes,' he said. 'But not here.' He looked around. 'We examine, we dissect. We take back evidence and information to stop our own people from getting sick. Far, far from here.'

'How far?' I breathed.

On the floor, Godfroi was stirring. His body was jerking and racked with pain. Even though he was a gaoler and a torturer, I still did not like to see it. And especially not on my rug.

'Can't you cure him?'

'Why?' said the Scientist dispassionately. 'He is not us. You too should use other animals to test your sicknesses on.'

I stared at him, puzzled. 'That's inhuman.'

'Correct. We are not human.'

'Are you…' I glanced out of the window at the suddenly deathly quiet streets that only a few days ago had been so crowded and choked with the colour of humanity; at Godfroi, moaning and writhing on the floor. This world… all I have seen of this world with its wars and its death and pointless cruelty… Oh, it feels done for me.

'Are you leaving now? To travel back to your own people?'

'When we have the samples we need.'

'Can…' I swallowed. 'Can we come with you?'

Wherever they go, I thought, it cannot be worse than traipsing so painfully slowly through the muck of this world.

They stopped, all three, together. Their beaks turned towards each other, curious. 'No disease carriers on the ship,' said one. 'Customs controls.'

'But an entire specimen,' said one. 'And it is free from disease. What could we not learn from it?'

'Patient Zero,' said the other.

They advanced towards me. I stayed stock still, as the huge beaks turned, and then sniffed loudly in my direction.

'A perfect specimen. What could we not infect her with?'

Their voices are rising in excitement.

'We could try everything… from someone as healthy as our own population!'

'And my children,' I said boldly.

Their beaks bobbed up and down excitedly. 'Better and better with the younglings. Are they all in good health?'

'There will… there will be experiments,' said the third, sealing his black bag with Godfroi's diseased arm in it.

I blinked. We would see about that. They could not hold me. I knew it. Nothing can.

And once we were free – away, in space, in the planets, in the many planets beyond this world – and I know there are legion, for I have sat, many, many nights, in the coldest mountains and the hottest deserts and I have tried to count them, and I cannot – I could fight, I could break them. They would not hold me. I would escape and be free, all of us together, riding the stars for ever.

'Take me.'

They were decided.

'We will take you.'

'Essie! Johann!' I shouted outside. 'Come. Our journey continues.'

'*BON!*' shouted Essie without hesitation, my bold girl.

And I knelt down and covered Godfroi, who was very near the end now. 'I'm sorry,' I said. 'I have to leave.'

He opened his pale terrified eyes. 'You, Dame of Misfortune. You brought this.'

'Nobody knows what brought it.'

'Will there… Do you think Hell is waiting for me?'

'Somewhere worse than Earth?' I said. 'I doubt it.'

'Let's go!' said Essie, bundling up her clothes. 'What is their food like?'

'Have they got big lights?' said Johann, his eyes wide. 'I like the big lights!'

We followed the figures outside. How strange to see the city deserted, from the great town houses, made of stone, to the lowliest hovel; everywhere, nothing but crosses on the doors, and quiet sobbing, a low field of lament, almost too quiet to hear, and a deep, lone voice, coming from far away: 'Bring out! Bring out your dead!'

But I was not sure there was anyone left here to bring out the dead, and they could not walk.

Behind the deserted baker's, its shingle tumbling down, we saw it, tucked in a stable; something black and shiny. In the shadows it was almost invisible, but as we got closer we saw it was a pointed ship, and we saw that it shone, that it was a strange metal I had never seen before.

'Ohhh!' said Johann and the baby on my back pointed out his little sticky finger.

'It's beautiful,' I said.

'You are ours,' they said.

'You think that,' I smiled politely.

The great door opened silently, lowered a plank, like a ship's, to the floor. My heart exulted. Inside was full of lights, as well as specimen boxes; an examination table and many other pieces of equipment I did not recognise. Some of it would work perfectly well as weapons. We were so ready.

'STOP!'

I turned at the noise. I should not have done.

It was Godfroi, stumbling, lurching, his remaining arm turning him into a travesty, his teeth bared like that of a man already dead. 'You did this to us!' he shouted, screamed at me. 'You came and infected us all.'

'No I didn't.'

'You are a Dame of Misfortune, I could see it all along.'

He was deranged. Best simply to leave.

'Let's go,' I said, quickly, to the bird men. 'Let's just go.'

Essie was almost at the gangplank. The baby was with me. Where was…

I turned round. Too late. Too late.

'Bye, friend,' my little curly-haired Johann was saying, right up at him. And Godfroi had him by the neck, and was starting to squeeze with his black and pustuled arm.

'You shall not keep him, Dame of Misfortune! And let all the misfortunes become yours!'

I trained for many years so none can best me on the field of battle. I am strong as ten men, through careful work; I can shoot an arrow through a bee and fell a dragoon. I have made myself the greatest fighter the world has ever known.

But that does not matter for this reason: the weakest, feyest mother ever born would have done without hesitation what I did next. In an instant. For that is simply what being a mother is.

I slew him with one clean blow of his own sword. The bird men looked on, silently. Johann was wiping his neck where that man had grabbed him, as Godfroi's blackened corpse dropped to the ground like an emptied sack, and I was glad.

I took Johann in my arms, although he was by rights getting too big to be lifted. Still nobody moved.

The bird man slowly sniffed the air with his huge beak. He brought up his large gloved hand and he pointed, steadily and slowly at Johann. Everyone stopped. Silence fell.

'That one,' he said. 'That one is still sick.'

'No,' I said. 'No, no, he's fine. He's had it. He's fine.'

Even as I could feel my beautiful boy's curls were stuck with sweat to his head.

'No living carriers,' said the other, pulling out his pointed light device. He flicked it on. My little boy was half worried, half delighted to see the light again.

'*Maman!*'

I froze, utterly horrified by what was unfolding in front of me. The shapes advanced on my boy.

But not for long. I grabbed Godfroi's filthy sword, and launched myself at the bird-like creature, a word on my tongue that was not French and not English but more ancient and coarse than both.

And I plunged it straight into the first beaked creature, without a thought for consequence or a thought at all except the blackest, bloodiest rage I had ever conceived of.

It was as I had perhaps suspected, but could not bring myself to believe: his leather-like garments were not leather, but instead his skin, tough as steel. I could not get purchase.

The other Scientists, though, did not come to his aid; they stood back, coolly observing, as the first thrashed his arm about – his strength was extraordinary – and suddenly his fingers uncoiled from what I had thought were gloves; they were in fact three times as long, like tentacles waving from his wrist, each pointed and sharp, and one pierced me in the chest like a needle, and I felt it as it started to draw blood from my body.

I screeched, and Essie grabbed Rue and ran back to the house, but Johann leapt forward and bit the Scientist hard on the leg, even as I screamed at him to stop, and that was just enough to startle the beast, and gave me enough time to jump back and pull out the needle, whereupon I swung my shoulders, as hard and as strongly as I ever had done anything; every second of training, every moment of battle was in it, as well as every ounce of fury that anyone would dare – *dare* – declare any of my children to be less than perfect, and I screamed and grunted and hacked and swore all the curses, and the arm of the Scientist, still twitching, the tentacles bouncing and open, was lying flat on the ground and he made a sound as crows do, when I shoot them from the trees with my bow without a second thought.

There was a terrible long silence settling in the tiny end of the baker's lane. I sensed sickening faces at windows. Then, from the Scientist I had wounded, more shrieking.

'Hellllp mmeeee,' he said, his huge head twisting, confused, as if he were trying to pick up his arm with the arm he no longer had.

I stood back, waiting, panting, but with my sword still held high. It was not covered in blood; rather something more glutinous and transparent.

'Helllp meeee.'

The first Scientist simply picked up the light pointer and immediately started to dissect the hand on the ground. The other brought his black bag, for taking back samples.

'Helllp meeee.'

The one with the light turned towards the Scientist on the ground. 'Now we shall examine the effects of pain on the spinal cortex.'

'Nooooo!'

'Stop!' I said.

'But this is Science,' they said.

Their injured comrade was now on the ground, contorted in pain. I knelt down by him.

'Our job is to rid our planet of disease,' he stuttered.

I nodded. 'By experimenting on others,' I said. 'So much for you.'

The buzzing of the light intensified. It was approaching.

'Tell me. Why do you think Johann is sick?' I said fiercely.

'I smell it,' said the Scientist. 'That is our beaks. We sniff out disease and injury and we work out how to stop it.'

'But you kill the person you experiment on?'

'Sometimes that is how Science works.'

'Didn't you think it was wrong?'

'Science has no right or wrong; only what is true.'

I blinked. 'What is wrong with Johann? He has had the sickness. He can't get it now.'

He shook his head. 'This disease doesn't work like that. This is something you can keep getting.'

I shook my head. 'But they seem better.'

The bird eyes blinked. 'They are trying to do their best. For you. But they are dead already.'

The light buzzed louder.

'As I am,' he said.

I lowered my head. 'What is it?'

'It is a simple disease. Carried by fleas, on rats.'

I shot up. Essie's rat. Godfroi had been right, curse him. 'No.'

'Don't leave me. Don't let me die alone.'

'You are not alone,' I said. 'You have your perfect brethren to tend you.'

The two other Scientists approached, and bent over him, with their needles and equipment and black bags; like doctors, yes. But much more like carrion crows.

I hurried back to our cottage. And there I saw that I should no longer fool myself. All the honey cakes, still there. Unfinished; barely touched. Sitting accusingly in a row. What child does not eat a honey cake, however old? Only a very, very sick one.

They were huddled together on the straw together; scared, as if they had done something wrong.

'*Maman*,' said Essie, quietly.

I stared at them; took in the stench of death that had settled; the stench all around of this godforsaken mud hole of a world and felt the end of everything; for everything I try is bad and wrong and gets worse; nothing will change, nothing will ever get better for me. And I am so tired of it, again and again and again, and I will not stand for it. No more. No.

NO.

Blinded, I ordered them to nap, then charged back outside, round the corner. The gleaming ship was still parked there. Of the first scientist there was almost nothing left; they had chopped him up and packed him away. But I didn't care about that, I did not care about him. I had absolutely nothing left to lose.

This entire filthy world had sickened and died on me. But I still had my knife and my sword.

'You must still take me,' I said boldly. 'To the stars.'

'Of course,' said one. 'We are always happy to have bodies donated to medical science.'

The two Scientists marched up their gangplank without looking behind them.

I looked behind at the once-bustling, now empty streets of a town I had barely got to know; where I had, running once again to escape, found nothing but the very bile of life.

Inside the ship, a buzz and a hum had started up and lights had started to sparkle inside the cabin in the most remarkable fashion, and the excitement built up in me, that finally, FINALLY I could leave it all behind me.

Yes of course I had loved them, but they were dead. They were dead.

'Wait for me!'

I will always remember this from the many battlefields I have traversed when the young men fell.

Whether French or Saxon or Nordic, their last words were always the same and they weren't, I should say, much about poetry, or death and glory and the magnificence of battle and their wonderful rewards in the afterlife.

As I stepped across the red fields and the bodies of the dying time after time wiping my blade, I heard them say only one thing, in different tongues: mother. *Mummy. Maman. Mutter. Madre, o Madre.*

They all, at the end, cried out for their mothers, like the little boys they were, with their big steel hats and their scarlet cloaks and their fancy horses.

You will all die, except for me.

You may die on the field of battle, or retching black bile helplessly in a room that reeks of the tannery, or without your mind in your own filth in a corner, staring at long ago.

There are no noble deaths. And most people – oh, you are so, so alone. So alone.

When you came into this world there were warm arms to greet you, to welcome you and hold you, to take you, and make you feel a part of this world, hold your flesh to the flesh whence you came; still your cries to the soft motion of your mother's heartbeat as she held you in her arms and promised over and over again how she would love you for as long as the moon and the stars.

But the moon and the stars are cold and do not care and last for ever. And when you leave the world, when you are undone, you will be alone: ripped on a foreign field, or under the hooves of a galloping horse, or sweating your life blood out, or babbling to yourself on a chair, the world disdaining to come near you, to warm your pallid, sinking flesh.

And you will want your mother.

I looked at the beautiful – and it was so, so beautiful, gleaming bright shiny metal – I looked at the beautiful ship once more.

The Scientists inside looked back at me, and cocked their strange heads.

The stink in our little home is deep now; the end is close. Rue is crying his little lungs out, but plaintively, not demanding; not in a way he thinks anyone will hear him. Essie is breathing in a shallow way, but trying to say, 'Rue, Rue, don't cry.' Johann simply stares at me, his eyes huge and mute in terror.

I feel once more around my neck. The tile is there of course. It is always there. The tile that shares immortality. Waiting to be given. I look from face to face.

I have tried to cut it. I have sharpened my knife, so many times. It will not cut. It cannot be shared.

Will it be my brave, my brilliant Essie? My sweet, my loving Johann? Or my laughing baby, whom I do not even know?

And then I think, 'It cannot be the baby. He would be a baby for ever.' And I look at my girl and my boy. And my heart, which has been kicked from palace to ditch, from shore to shore, is stabbed anew. And I am looking at my girl and my boy. My girl and my boy.

I step forward, lifting the tile up and away from my body. I tear my eyes away from my beautiful tousle-headed boy, who is gazing at me. I cannot. I cannot look at him. I take one more step towards Ess, my skin crawling with horror at what I am about to do.

Then suddenly Essie groans in deep pain. And I freeze and shudder. I do not know how this alien magic I carry works, nor what it is supposed to do.

What if… what if it freezes her, not just as a child, but as a sick child? What if it keeps her in this foul state for ever? Could one imagine a worse torture?

My hand flies to my mouth in horror. I stare at the tile. I was in good health when he did what he did to me.

Oh, for all the times I have been tried as a witch: if I only could, truly, curse the man who did this to me, if I could pull his blood out across the stars, slowly, drop by drop whilst he screamed the heavens apart, then I would.

I let the tile fall slowly back against my skin and heave a great sigh.

'*Maman?*' says Essie, her voice trembling.

I sit on the damp straw bed, pick up the baby, who quietens immediately and nuzzles into my neck, the way his head is designed to fit so perfectly there. And I gather Johann in one crook of my elbow, and Essie just about manages, pale and weary as she is, to lie on the other.

'What's happening?' says Essie, as weak as if she is waking from a dream.

'You are going…' I say. 'On a journey. Like on the boat. But where you are going there will be no sickness and no pain.'

'Will you be with us, *Maman*?' says Johann, croaking. His little hands are pinned tightly around my waist.

I take the deepest of breaths. 'Listen to me. I will be with you every single second. My arms will be around you and I will be loving you and you will never ever think for a second of your life that you were not utterly beloved, every single bit of you, everything you ever were from the moment I knew you were coming; everything you ever did, everything you ever were or could ever be, was wonderful and perfect in my eyes. You were so beloved, and you made me so very, very happy. The happiest I have ever been in my whole life, and the happiest I will ever be, and I am so very, very proud of you and I am always here for you, every single second.'

His little face relaxes and he smiles. 'Was I good?'

'You were so very much better than good.'

'I am so tired, *Maman*.'

'Sleep a while,' I say.

The baby is already quiet. Oh, he is so very quiet. Essie's head is heavy on my arm. Her dark soft hair lies across my skin.

'Sweet *Maman*, sing,' she says, her eyelashes fluttering across her downy cheek, every freckle on it something I have made, worshipped, adored; every single beat of her, and I should, I will not regret a single moment, and the infinity of howling misery that blows the carved wooden door to eternal winter open in front of me, well, shall we say that it was worth it?

'Rough blows the North Wind, cruel blows the East'

This tiny gap of light you opened for me, you three, in my infinity of dark; that tiniest moment of sunshine: shall we say then that the thousand thousand days of misery are worth the three cooling heads at my breast, shall we?

'Heavy blows the South Wind, we all fall beneath…'

Of course, of course we shall… it was worth it and I will pay for it willingly, every second: oh my loves, oh my loves, how you were loved how I loved.

August 24th

August 25th

August 26th

August 27th

I knotted Essie's plaited hair tight around my wrist as my warrior's totem and set out just after dawn. There was panic in the city now, you could feel it; the disease spreading everywhere. It was a beautiful morning too.

They were burying the corpses beyond the city walls. I looked in pity at the men who took this work; who provided some accompaniment, at least, at the end, when the finest and the great and rich ladies and gentlemen had fled in short order. I did not think they would escape it. Rich and poor, we all end the same, for I have been both. Except of course I do not end. But the having of children. That has ended.

And here and there I saw shapes that startled me: the belief that the bird-men were indeed physicians has stayed strong, for those who do care, those who have agreed to help tend the sick; they now wear the great beaked masks, to show what they do.

I passed one on his way through the fields, who nodded.

'Rather you than me,' I said, for I was trying out myself anew, and feel the need now to only ever be light.

He shrugged.

'My money is on the rat fleas,' I said, as cheerily as I could. And I heard his mask move, and I felt his eyes on me as I carried on down the road; but I did not turn my head, for looking back is over for me now: and also, I had no wish to see his face.

The Ghosts of Branscombe Wood

Justin Richards

I have had so many names I don't remember them all. I have been Ash and I have been Alys. I have been Lady Sherade and Lady Electra, and even a queen. Once, so long ago I can barely recall it, I was Ashildr. But now I have given up trying to remember what I am called. I remember only who I am. I am Me. That is the only name I need.

The minutes, the hours, the days come and go. The years pass and so – all too soon – do the centuries. I remember when it was 1400. I remember thinking how long it had been since I left my home village. And now, all too soon, 1600 has come and gone...

The air has a smell, almost a taste, imbued by the recent rain. Once I would have marvelled at it, and let it pervade my senses. Now I find it as stale and unremarkable as everything else in this slow-changing world. Everything changes, except me. Everything grows old and passes away, crumbles to dust, except me. Or rather, Me.

I am travelling again. But this time, I am looking for somewhere to settle, to make my home. For how long, I know not. Years perhaps. Decades. Centuries. I have wealth enough to purchase a plot of land and a fine house. It is just a question of finding the right place. My possessions and wealth – and all my other journals (so many of them) I have left in the safe keeping of someone I know in London. I would call him a friend, but all too soon he will be gone like everyone else. I do not make friends now, because I cannot bear to lose them. I have so much, but I have lost so much more.

I had not travelled far from London. I think I want to stay close to the city, although I no longer wish to live within its confines. My rather rudimentary map called the area Branscombe.

The road narrowed to a track and this disappeared into a wood. Another track led off around the trees. I pulled on the reins to slow my horse, and consulted the map again. The route around the wood was far longer than the distance through it, and there appeared to be nothing along the way that made the longer path interesting. So I folded the map and put it away, then urged the horse forward again, towards the trees.

Before long, we were swallowed up by the wood. Sunlight scattered across the ground where it could break through the canopy of leaves. The horse had slowed to a walk, but I was in no hurry. Other, narrower paths split off but I kept to the main track as it led me deeper into the shadows.

I had been travelling for perhaps an hour when I saw the knight.

He stood at a junction where another narrow path led off from the track I was following. What light made it through the green canopy above us was reflected off his polished breastplate as he stood silent and impassive and utterly incongruous. As I approached, he raised a gauntleted hand to stop me.

I could see now that his armour was of an old design. In fact, it looked identical to a suit of armour I had seen before. But that was in another country and long ago. For a moment, in my mind's eye I imagined I saw the knight who wore that armour charging towards me again. He was mounted on a snow-white horse, galloping towards our ranks on the field of Agincourt.

But that knight was long gone. He would have died of old age well over a century ago, if my arrow hadn't struck the weak point below his helmet, penetrated his armour, and killed him in an instant. I forget how many I killed that day, but as I saw the figure standing before me, I remembered the knight on his white charger…

'What do you want, sir knight?' I called out as my horse approached.

'You must take another path,' he replied. His voice was muffled by his helmet, the visor down. Even so, I could hear his French accent.

'This is the most direct route,' I told him. 'This path takes me through the wood to the village of Branscombe.' I had half a mind to take out the map and show him.

But at my words, the knight drew his sword. It was obvious he did not intend to move, and my bow and arrows were long gone.

'This path leads to death,' the knight said. 'I tell you again – take another.'

For several moments we faced each other. I looked down at him from my horse, and contemplated simply riding on and letting him try to stop me. From his stance, I had no doubt that he would try. And if he was telling the truth and some danger did indeed lurk ahead, then he was right to warn me away.

So, finally, I pulled on the reins, and directed the horse onto the narrower path.

'You have chosen well,' the knight called after me.

I did not reply, but raised my hand in acknowledgement. When I did look back, as the path turned and headed deeper into the wood, the knight was gone.

It was difficult to know how long I was in the wood. Time seemed to stand still in the eerie, shadowy domain. I measured it out by the steps of the horse. Its hooves on the path supplied a drumbeat accompaniment to the beating of my heart and the pulse of my breathing. But finally, the trees thinned and the sunlight brightened. The patches of shadow grew smaller as the puddles of light enlarged and I emerged into daylight.

My eyes had adjusted gradually to the brightness as the wood petered out. I found myself on a gently sloping hillside leading down into a wide valley. In the distance I could see a river and on its banks a small settlement made up of several dozen houses. Smoke rose from what I guessed was a blacksmith's.

As I approached the village I saw the people. At first there were just a few. But gradually the numbers grew as villagers came out into the streets and stared up at me. They watched as my horse made its way down the path towards them – young and old, men and women. It was as if they'd never seen a woman riding a horse before.

But, as I discovered when I reached the village and they cautiously welcomed me, it was not who I was that intrigued them. It was where I had come from.

A young lad took my horse to find it water and a pasture or stable. I forget his name or rather, to be honest, I made no effort to remember it. Perhaps he never told me, although he asked me the name of the horse. I had to admit it didn't have a name. He seemed surprised at this. But I know from experience that if I name something then I miss it all the more when it is gone.

While my horse was tended to, I was invited into the house of the man I assumed was in charge of the village. Perhaps they had a Head Man, or perhaps he was simply the most respected citizen. He was middle-aged, his face craggy and his hair greying and thinning. His name I do recall – it was Edward. He offered me ale, apologising that there was nothing more refined for a lady of my obvious standing. But I am as happy to drink ale as I am the finest wine.

His wife, Maria, brought two tankards. She had weathered better than her husband and I could still see how pretty she must once have been. 'You came from the wood,' Edward said, almost as soon as we had sat down.

'I came *through* the wood,' I corrected him. 'My journey started long before that.' I did not tell him how many centuries before…

Edward nodded. 'Of course. Forgive our surprise, but no one from the village ever ventures into the wood. Or very rarely.'

'Really?' I told him I found this hard to believe, especially as the path through the wood afforded the shortest distance to the nearest town.

'You're right. It is a great inconvenience to have to go round the wood to get to the market rather than cutting through it.'

'So why do you not go through the wood?' I asked.

'You had no trouble on your journey?' He took a swig of ale. 'You saw… nothing unusual?'

I thought of my brief encounter with the knight. But I decided not to mention that. At least, not until I discovered what he was talking about. So I shook my head. 'It was a pleasant ride.'

He frowned. 'Then you were very lucky, my lady.' He took another drink, as if considering what to say. 'The woods,' he told me at last, 'are haunted.' He smiled apologetically, as if to say, 'I know it sounds incredible, but it really is not my fault.'

Being more used to incredible things than he was, I merely nodded and smiled. 'Haunted in what way?' I asked.

'People who venture into the woods see things. People. Dead people they know, or used to know. Other things too. Strange lights, eerie sounds…'

He paused to drain his tankard and signalled to his wife for her to refill it. Even in the dim light within the house I could see he had grown pale.

'I met a knight,' I told him.

'A knight?'

'A French knight, judging by his accent. But I saw no one else.'

'And this knight did not attack you?'

'No. But,' I admitted, 'he did give me a warning.'

'He sent you away on a different path to the one you wished to take,' Edward said. It was a statement rather than a question, and I nodded. 'They do that,' he said. 'You did well to heed the warning.'

'And if I had not?'

'Those who do not heed the advice of the apparitions, those who venture where the spirits tell them they should not…' He broke off and I saw him shiver. 'Finish your ale,' he said, accepting the full tankard his wife handed him. 'Let us talk for a while of other things. And then, when you are done, I shall show you what happens if you ignore the warnings.'

I was intrigued, but one thing I have learned in the long, lonely, empty years is patience. So I happily talked of my journey, of how things were in London, of rumours that the Queen was ailing. She was, after all, very old, Edward said. I smiled and did not reply.

When we had finished our ale, Edward led me outside. We made our way through the village. The people seemed to be going about their normal business, the novelty of a woman who had come through the woods already wearing off. I passed my horse, tied up outside the blacksmith's and drinking water from a wooden trough. I patted him gently on the flank and he nodded his head in acknowledgement.

We came at last to a house near the edge of the village. A man and woman, about the same age as Edward, came out as we approached. He went to speak to them briefly, asking me to wait a moment. The man and woman looked at me as he spoke. They frowned, but nodded, then stood aside and Edward beckoned for me to join him. Together we went into the house.

Another woman sat at the table, staring straight ahead. She was much younger, about the same age as I look.

'This is Jane,' Edward said. 'Her parents kindly agreed that we could see her.'

'Hello, Jane,' I said.

But the young woman did not acknowledge me. She continued to stare into space, as if we were not there.

'Can she hear me?' I wondered. 'Can she see me?'

Edward sighed. 'I cannot say for certain. I believe she can, though she chooses not to.'

'But why?' I asked.

'When she was a child,' Edward explained, 'she got lost in the woods. As far as we can tell, she ignored the ghosts and ventured where they told her not to. You know what children are like.'

I nodded. I knew all too well. And now that my eyes adjusted to the gloom, I could see that Jane's face was relaxed and her eyes wide like a child's.

'Since then she has been like this,' Edward went on. 'Whatever she saw drove her out of her mind. She spends most of her time staring at things that are not there. She rarely speaks, and when she does it is single words. At most a short sentence. She has never spoken about what happened to her or what she saw in the woods.'

As he spoke, Jane turned and looked at me. Her mouth twitched slightly into the hint of a smile. In that moment, I saw something in her demeanour. I don't know what it was. Perhaps her expression, perhaps the vague smile. But I saw something that reminded me of my own daughter Essie. And in that moment, I knew that whatever ghosts, spirits, or apparitions haunted Branscombe Wood I was determined to exorcise them.

*

I spent the night in a spare room in Edward and Maria's house. It was cold and a little damp, and the wind crept through a crack between the window and its frame. But the mattress was softer than the hard ground I had slept on for the past few nights. I woke early as the first light of the day edged into the room. Even before I opened my eyes, I knew it was sunny.

I lay there for a while, listening to the sounds of the village waking up. People were moving. In the house below, Maria – I assumed – was in the kitchen. I could hear the sheep in a nearby pasture and watched the light move slowly across the floor as the sun moved higher in the sky.

And all the while, I wondered how best to deal with the ghosts. Edward had told me that different people saw different things. The only constant seemed to be that the apparitions warned against taking certain paths. Whatever had befallen Jane, it had happened because she failed to heed the warnings. Perhaps she was too young to understand them when she ventured into the woods and got lost. Or perhaps she ignored them simply out of the contrariness of youth. But whatever the reason, she had gone where the apparitions forbade her to go, and she had suffered a terrible fate – a shock or a fright – as a result.

This, then, was the key. In order to unlock the mystery of the ghosts and discover how they might be banished for ever from Branscombe Wood, I needed to ascertain what they were protecting. Or at least, as a first step along that path, I needed to discover where within the wood they wanted to keep sacrosanct.

Edward was understandably wary as I explained my plan to him over breakfast. It was a simple meal of bread and cheese, but it was more than enough to satisfy me. We talked long after we had finished eating and Maria had cleared away the plates.

'Don't you see,' I said when we had been round and round the same arguments several times, 'this is a chance. It's a chance not only to discover what happened to poor Jane, but also to regain the woods. If we can banish the ghosts for good, then you won't have to take a long detour round them to get to market. You won't have to worry about letting your children play there. It may be,' I admitted, 'that after we have learned what or where the apparitions are guarding, we are unable to rid ourselves of them. But at least you will have tried. Surely it is better to try and fail than not to try at all.'

We argued some more, but I think that was the turning point. He could see the merit of my argument, and finally Edward agreed to talk to some of the other villagers.

'What I'm suggesting isn't dangerous,' I stressed. 'It's merely finding out the truth. I'm not asking you or the other villagers to do anything you haven't already done. But this time we can make use of it.'

With Edward persuaded, the other villagers offered only token resistance. Before long, I was unfolding my map of the area on the same table where Edward, Maria and I had eaten our bread and cheese. With the help of the villagers I was able to add some details to the map. Together we traced out the various paths through the woods, or at least the ones they knew about.

That done, I told them what I proposed. They listened in silence, occasionally nodding in agreement. It was fairly simple. We would go into the woods, each taking an allocated path. As soon as we saw one of the ghosts, we would leave.

But everyone needed to take careful note of where they were when the apparition appeared to them – and of where the ghost did not want them to go.

Several of the villagers decided to go in pairs. Others, those either more brave or more foolhardy, were happy to go into the haunted woods alone. But the important thing was that we had enough groups to cover each of the paths. With everyone allocated their own route, we nervously shook hands. And I confess I was probably as nervous as any of them, because I knew that if harm came to any of the villagers then it would be solely and heavily on my conscience.

It was with a sense of shared trepidation that we made our way towards the woods. I admit that I also felt a keen anticipation, a thrill of excitement at the prospect of discovering more about the so-called ghosts of Branscombe Wood.

I walked with Edward and Maria to the point just within the woods where our paths diverged. I could see the apprehension in both their faces, though they tried to hide it, as we said our goodbyes. Then they turned and walked briskly along their path, hand in hand like teenaged lovers. I allowed myself a smile. Was I perhaps just a little envious of their love, of the fact that they each had someone to share their life? Perhaps I was. But I put aside all such thoughts and turned to start along my own path.

They told me later what they had seen, gathered again in Edward and Maria's house a few hours later, and I listened to all their stories.

A few – a very few – had encountered no apparitions, no strange figures, and continued along their path until it finally emerged on the far side of the wood. But most had been warned away. Each person, it seemed, had encountered someone appropriate to themselves. Even those who walked together did not always see the same figure, warning them away from the path they had taken.

One woman had seen the long-dead grandfather she remembered from when she was a child. She described his stature and expression, the lined face and wrinkled hands as he warned her away. A man haltingly described his meeting with his wife – dead for just over a month. The tears welled up in his eyes as he told us in a cracked and emotional voice of meeting her at a junction of his path and another. He had tried to go to her, to embrace her, he said. But she had backed away, shaking her head. That more than anything seemed to affect him.

A younger couple struggled to keep their composure as they admitted they had met the daughter they had lost over a year ago. The young girl had called out to them, laughed and smiled just as they remembered. You can never forget the sound of your children's laughter, the mother told us. I turned away at that, afraid that my own expression would betray the fact that I knew all too well that this was true.

Edward and Maria had each seen different figures. They heard the same words, the same warnings. But Edward heard them from his long-dead father. Maria from her older sister, who died before she was twenty. I felt a moment of pride at how they both kept their emotions in check.

When they asked me what I had seen, I told them that it was the same knight as I had encountered before. There was nothing to be gained from telling them the truth.

Not that I lied to them, because I did see that same knight. This time, I ignored his warning, walking right up to him. So close I could see the holes in his armour that my arrows had made. As I reached him, the knight vanished. And another figure appeared, a little further along the path.

My heart skipped a beat as I saw the long mask jutting out from the man's face. A mask I knew only too well. He was a plague doctor. In fact, I was certain he was a plague doctor who had attended my children in their sickness.

'Death lies this way,' he said. His voice echoed slightly, distorted by the mask. 'Do not risk your life by coming further down the path. Turn aside while you still can.'

But, whether out of bravery or stubbornness, I continued.

'I warn you – stop!'

As I reached the man, I fancied I could smell the plague on him. The sickly stench of death and decay. And then he too was gone, and another figure stepped out of the shadows and onto the path ahead of me.

'Turn aside,' he commanded.

I stopped abruptly. The man's face was shadowed beneath his helmet and so he could have been any of a dozen or more of the Viking men from the village where I had grown up.

He took a step towards me, his face still concealed. 'This is not a path you should take. Even you are not immune to the horrors that lie ahead if you continue.'

I would like to say that I continued down the path. I would like to say that I braved him out, and he too disappeared as I went on my way. But in truth, this sudden confrontation with my own childhood, with all that happened to me so long ago, was too much. I turned and ran back the way I had come.

But, as I said, I told Edward and the other villagers nothing of this. I merely described the knight of Agincourt once more. They wanted to know how I knew the knight, how he was relevant to me as their own apparitions were personal to them. I told them vaguely of being caught at the edge of a battle while travelling in France. I said I had seen the knight die. I did not say that it was almost two hundred years ago, or that it was I who had killed him.

To discourage any further discussion, I unfolded the map once more on Edward and Maria's table.

'You want us to show you where we each saw our ghost,' Edward said.

I nodded. 'If we mark the sightings on the map, then that may give us some clue as to their purpose,' I told them. 'Perhaps we will discern a pattern of some sort. We shall see.'

So, one by one, they showed me the point on the map where they had encountered the ghost. I marked each position clearly on the map with a cross. It took a while, as each and every person was keen to recount their own adventure. We all listened patiently, and as the light dimmed and evening drew in, it became clear to me that it would be another day before we could progress further with our investigations and exorcism.

Finally, as Maria lit the candles round the edge of the room and I struggled to make out the detail of the map in the gloom, the last of the encounters was reported. I drew a cross at the relevant point. We agreed to meet again in the morning and examine the map to see what we could deduce from our day's work. But, in truth, I had already seen all there was to see. I had discerned the pattern that had emerged when we were but halfway through plotting the positions of the apparitions.

And so I was somewhat preoccupied as Maria served the evening meal. I did my best to seem interested in Maria and Edward's conversation. They were keen to talk again about what they had seen in the woods, and also to question me about what our next stratagem could or should be.

But I kept my own counsel, and did not reveal what I had deduced. For one thing, I wanted to see the map in daylight to be absolutely sure I was right. For another, I wanted to ponder some more on how to approach the problem of the ghosts. But if I was right, then at least we had some focus for our attentions.

I retired early, wanting to spend some time alone considering the matter. But in fact I soon slipped into a deep sleep. I did not awaken from it until the sun had been risen for several hours. But I felt refreshed. And as I washed and dressed and made my way downstairs, I knew that really there was only one course of action open to us.

The villagers who had been brave enough to venture into the woods the previous day gathered again at Edward and Maria's house. Once more I unfolded the map on the table. I had already unfolded it on the floor of my small room upstairs to check that I was not mistaken in what I thought I had seen. It was even more clear than I had imagined. So I was confident not only that I had something to tell them, but also that they would easily see it for themselves.

'These crosses,' I reminded everyone as they stood round expectantly, 'show the places where we all saw the ghosts in Branscombe Wood yesterday.' I pointed to them in turn as I spoke. 'I think they form a pattern. A pattern that tells us why the ghosts appear.'

I let this sink in as the villagers leaned forward, straining to get a better view of the map. I waited a few moments, but when no one spoke, I went on:

'They form a ring,' I explained. 'Not a perfect circle, because the apparitions appear at points where they can persuade whoever they meet onto another path. But look.'

I drew a line through the crosses, forming a better circle than I had expected.

'So how does that help?' one of the villagers asked.

'That was what I wondered,' I said, biting back the impulse to comment on the man's evident stupidity.

'Does it mean that the ghosts emanate from somewhere within that ring?' Edward suggested.

'I think it does,' I agreed. 'But I also think there's more to it than that. What do the ghosts do?' I prompted.

'They turn us aside from our chosen paths,' Maria answered.

'And why would they do that?' I asked.

'Because they don't want us to go that way,' another villager said.

I nodded. 'So let's look at the ways they don't want us to go.' I pointed to the various paths, each marked with a cross. 'And they all lead into this ring.'

'It's as if the ghosts are a fence around that area,' a young woman said. 'Like a fence round a field.'

'Exactly,' I agreed. 'But we would put a fence round a field to keep cattle or horses or sheep inside. This fence…' I pointed again at the map. 'This fence is there to keep people *out*.'

'But why?' another man asked.

'Because,' I said, 'I believe there is something in that area that the ghosts don't want anyone to see. Something they are protecting. Or rather, something that is using the ghosts to protect itself.'

There was a short silence as they all considered this.

'So, what do you suggest we do?' Edward asked at last.

'Well, I don't know about the rest of you,' I said, 'but I'd like to know what it is they don't want us to see. So I suggest we go and take a look.'

'Past the ghosts?' Maria asked.

'But they want to keep us out,' someone else said.

'She is right,' Edward said. 'If we want to get rid of the ghosts, we need to know why they are there. And it seems there is only one way to find that out.'

'I can't make any of you come with me,' I told them. 'But I intend to go to the area inside that ring I've drawn on the map, and see what is there.'

'No one's ever been there,' the young man who had lost his daughter said.

'Jane has,' his wife said quietly. 'And we all know what happened to her.'

'Then we must go there to stop it happening to anyone else,' I countered.

There were some muttered agreements.

'Look,' I told them, 'anyone who isn't happy venturing into the woods again can go home now. But anyone who wants to help, come with me. If when we see the ghosts again it becomes too much of an ordeal, then leave. Come home, back to the village. But if we can get to the centre of the ring, then perhaps – and I make no promises – but *perhaps* we can rid the wood of these apparitions. We can make sure no one else suffers like Jane has.'

I stepped back, allowing them to talk amongst themselves for a while. Several of the villagers left almost at once. A few more drifted away during their discussions. Finally, only half a dozen villagers remained.

I was pleased to see that Edward had stayed, although he had spoken quietly to Maria and sent her out to the back room. I sensed that she would have joined us if her husband had permitted it. I could not blame him for wanting to keep her safe. Similarly, the young man who had lost his daughter had also stayed with us, but his wife had gone. I suspected that he too had sent her away, desperate to keep her safe whatever fate might befall him.

'Thank you,' I said to them.

Dark clouds were gathering in the sky as we set off, perhaps presaging what lay ahead for us. There was little conversation as we made our way out of the village and up the hill towards the wood.

Rather than split up again, we had decided that this time strength lay in numbers. We would stay together, taking the most direct path through the woods to the area that the ghosts seemed determined to prevent us from entering. I had told everyone before we set off that if the apparitions became too much for them, then there was no dishonour in turning away and returning to the village. I told them this again as we entered the woods. Somewhere in the distance there was a rumble of thunder, punctuating my words.

I probably felt as apprehensive as any of the others as we started along the path. They tried to hide it, but I could see the anxiety etched across the villagers' faces, and I was sure my own face told much the same story.

I cannot say what the others saw. I imagine that we all saw a figure at the same time, standing ahead of us on the path. But it was clear from their reactions that what the others saw was not what appeared to me. It was something personal, relevant, taken from their own past. Just as the knight from Agincourt – now more familiar from my encounters with him in the wood than from the field of battle almost two centuries earlier – was to me.

'It isn't real,' I said, as much for my own benefit as anyone else's. 'Whatever you see, remember that it isn't real. It can't harm you.'

'No?' one of the men said quietly. He was a tall man, with a bushy red beard. But his eyes betrayed his fear. 'Remember what happened to poor Jane.'

'She was a child,' Edward told him. 'What happened to her was all within her mind. No one laid a finger on her.'

'That's right,' I agreed. 'The only danger is inside our own minds.'

I'm not sure he was convinced, but we all walked on together, ignoring the knight – or whatever anyone else saw – as he gestured for us to move aside and take another path.

The figure vanished as we reached it, fading into the shadows and becoming insubstantial until there was nothing left. At once the mood of the group lifted. Someone laughed. We walked on, apparently with more confidence now that this first obstacle had been overcome.

But the confidence was not to last.

We had not travelled much further along the path when the next apparition appeared before us. Just as the previous one had melted away into the air, this new figure seemed to congeal out of the shadows as it gained form and substance. Again, I do not know what the others saw. But Edward crossed himself and muttered what I assumed was a prayer.

Again, for me it was a familiar figure – the otherworldly plague doctor who had diagnosed my dying children. Even when he was fully formed before me, he seemed strangely vague, his outline blurred and indistinct. It took me several moments to realise that this was because I was seeing him through the tears that were welling up in my eyes. Whatever was producing these apparitions, it knew how to find a knife to its victims' hearts. And then, having plunged it in deep, how to twist it.

Whatever he saw was too much for the man with the red beard. 'I'm sorry,' he stammered, then turned and walked briskly away. A few moments later, another man followed him, together with a young woman.

'Are you all right?' Edward asked me.

I realised he must be able to see the tears glistening on my cheeks. I wiped them away with my sleeve and nodded. 'Of course. Are you?'

'I think so,' he replied, and I could hear the tremor in his voice. I was tempted to ask him what he could see, but I feared that might just make it worse for him.

'We go on,' I said firmly, and I took hold of Edward's trembling hand. Together we stepped towards the figure on the path, only dimly aware of the others following.

Again the figure melted away as we reached it. But our numbers were now depleted. There were just two other villagers left besides Edward and myself. One was the young man who had seen his dead daughter. The other was a middle-aged woman with a round face which I imagined was more used to smiling than the anxiety it now portrayed.

As the next figure began to form out of the heavy air, the woman gave a yelp of horror. The young man sank to his knees, his hands covering his face. The woman backed away a few paces, then turned and ran.

Edward's face was pale and drawn. He turned away from the apparition and went to the young man, putting his hand on the man's shoulder. He leaned down and spoke quietly. I had no doubt that he was telling the man to leave us and go home to his wife. Sure enough the man got slowly to his feet, looked at me with wide, terrified eyes, then turned, and hurried after the woman.

In front of us, the figure pointed, gesturing for us to turn aside. I have no idea what Edward saw, but it affected him deeply. For myself, it was an effort to put one foot in front of the other. 'It isn't real,' I said to myself over and over. '*She* isn't real.' But every halting, fearful step took me a pace closer to my own dead infant daughter.

It was all I could do not to sink to my knees and weep. I felt Edward take my hand, and together we stumbled onwards. I wanted to close my eyes, but I could not look away from the figure that I knew so well, that I remembered so desperately. It seemed to take for ever, although in truth it must have been only a few seconds. But finally we reached the figure.

Essie looked at me, an expression of sadness mixed with disappointment on her face. Then she shook her head. 'Mother,' she breathed. 'Oh, Mother.' Or perhaps I imagined the words. In another moment, she was gone. But I knew the memory of that moment would haunt me for as long as the memory of her death...

'I'm sorry,' Edward said. He gripped my hand tighter, pulling gently so I had to turn towards him.

'I'm sorry too,' I said. 'If what you saw was half as upsetting as what I saw...'

But he was shaking his head. 'That's not what I meant. It just gets worse. Every time is worse than the time before, harder than the time before.'

'Which must mean we are getting closer to our goal,' I pointed out.

Edward shook his head again, and I realised that there were tears running down his wrinkled cheeks. 'I can't do that again,' he said. 'We tried. We did our best. But I think we must stop now.'

'But we're so close,' I said. 'We must be close.'

'Even so.'

I could tell from his tone, from his expression, from the tight grip on his hand, from the way he stood – from everything about him – that he was right. Edward could go no further. And somehow that made me even more determined to discover the truth about the ghosts of Branscombe Wood.

'You go home,' I said gently. 'Go back to Maria. Stay safe.'

He frowned as he realised what I meant. 'But, are you not coming too?'

I tried to force a smile. Whether it looked anything like a smile or merely served to show how scared I really was I have no idea. 'I will go on.' I let go of his hand, and pressed my forefinger to his lips to stop him protesting. 'I've come this far, and I think I can go a little further at least. If I don't,' I told him, 'then all this has been for nothing.'

Edward nodded slowly. 'I can see that,' he said quietly. 'I'm sorry I can't stay with you.'

'Don't be,' I told him. 'Go back to Maria. Stay safe with her. You both have far more to lose than I have.' He looked at me quizzically, and I spoke before he could ask: 'I have already lost everything I ever had,' I said quietly. 'Many times over. Don't ask. Just go.'

He reached out and took my hand again. For a moment, he held it tight, then he pressed it to his lips, nodded, let go of my hand and turned and walked quickly away. Perhaps he paused. Perhaps he looked back. I do not know, because I was already walking down the path, towards the next ghost.

As the figure fleshed out in front of me, congealing out of shadow and darkness, I knew that this would be the last ghost I would have to face on my journey. Whoever or whatever was doing this had reached back into my mind and memory as far as I myself could remember to conjure this particular apparition.

A figure I barely remembered stood ahead waiting for me on the path. I had all but forgotten what he looked like, but I knew at once who he was. He was the man – if man he be – who had been responsible for my death all those years ago. Centuries ago. And in causing my death, he had condemned me to this unending life. Condemned me to watch those I love and care for fade and slip away – like ghosts, but far more real.

I bit hard into my lower lip, hoping the physical pain of it would blot out the emotional pain. I did look back then, hoping that somehow Edward had changed his mind and was still there with me. But he had gone. I turned back, alone, to face Odin.

He stared back at me, one eye covered as I remembered, dressed in the trappings of the god that he was not and never had been. Even in life,

Odin had been a deception I told myself. He was not what he seemed then, and he was not what he seemed now.

'Stand aside, woman,' he commanded. He raised his hand, palm out, to stop me.

I hesitated. I desperately wanted to do as he said, to turn away. To run back to the village and tell them I had done the best I could, and that I was sorry it was not enough. But I knew it wasn't true. I could do more. I could go on.

'This is your last chance, Ashildr,' Odin said. I think what shocked me most was the sound of my name – my real name from so long ago. 'You do not wish to see what lies ahead.'

So, I thought, there *is* something ahead – I was right. And that moment of elation – that moment of knowing that this was not all for nothing and that there was indeed something to be discovered inside that area protected by the ghosts – that spurred me on. I realised with surprise that I was smiling. And this time it was a real, genuine smile and not a mask to hide my true feelings.

'No,' I said, my voice strong and confident. 'You who are not Odin, and who never was – *you* stand aside.'

I stood for a moment in front of him, staring into his face. Then I raised my hand and pushed him away.

Except that my hand touched nothing but the empty air where Odin had been standing. I was alone again on the path. And I knew that I had almost reached my destination. Whatever it might be.

My heart thumping hard in my chest, I took a deep breath and continued along the path. Was it my imagination, or had the shadows deepened? As if in answer there was a rumble of thunder. Through the dense canopy of trees, what I could see of the sky had darkened to a metallic grey. It was just a coincidence of course, but it unsettled me.

Ahead of me, the path curved gently through the trees so that where it led was hidden. But as I started along the curved section, I could see something glistening in the pale light ahead of me. I could not yet make it out, but it looked like a metal structure of some sort.

As I grew closer I saw that many of the trees and bushes that I had assumed masked the structure from me were in fact growing up into it. Whatever this strange building was, it had been here for so long that the wood was growing through it as well as around it.

The building looked more like a castle than anything else I had seen before. It was made of metal, dulled and tarnished with age. A central tower rose to a pointed turret, while the lower part splayed out into a larger shape. Buttresses projected out from the base, bent and rusted. The bottom of the huge castle looked as though it had been burned, the metal bubbled and charred by intense heat.

I stood for a while, staring at the strange castle. Was this what the ghosts and apparitions were guarding? And if so, what could be inside? Of course, there was only one way to find out and I could put off the moment no longer. From where I stood there was no obvious entrance to the castle. In fact, now I looked, I could see no windows either. The only holes in the building were where the branches of trees had forced their way through.

As I warily circled the castle, I saw that one large tree trunk had broken through the side of the castle, branches hanging down the outside. Moss and ivy grew across the dented metal. Further round, I finally saw what I had been looking for – a way in.

The arched entrance was covered by a metal door. I could see no sign of any handle or lock. The metal seemed completely smooth, except for a patina of rust and corrosion. I looked round for a bell-pull or doorknocker as I approached, but could see neither. But then, as I grew closer – close enough to reach out and touch this weird door – it slid open before me. The metal door retracted into the frame, leaving an open archway.

I hesitated on the threshold. Inside was only darkness. I listened but apart from the wind in the trees and another distant roll of thunder I could hear nothing. Certainly no sound came from within. Feeling every bit as disconcerted as when I had seen the ghosts, I stepped inside.

Immediately, the interior flickered into light. It was a dull glow, tinged red. But I could see no sign of either candles or oil lamps. The light seemed to come from everywhere and nowhere. What it illuminated was a passageway stretching ahead of me. Even in this dull, blood-red light, I could see that the walls inside the castle were also metal, as was the floor. I looked up, and was not surprised to see that the ceiling too gleamed dully. A strand of ivy hung down where it had forced its way through an imperceptible crack high above.

My feet rang on the floor as I walked slowly along the corridor, the sound echoing off the metal walls. Ahead of me, more light glimmered into life, as if sensing that I was there.

A noise from behind made me stop and turn abruptly. I saw that the metal door had slid shut behind me, and I hoped that it would open as mysteriously when I returned. *If* I returned, I thought, not having any idea what might lie ahead. I started forward again, and I sensed rather than saw that, just as light appeared ahead of me, so it was extinguished behind me. When I did glance over my shoulder, the end of the corridor and the door where I had entered were lost in darkness.

I wondered for the first time what I would do if there was nothing here. What if this was all there was to find – this metal castle with its strange door and eerie light? How far should I go before I turned back, before I returned to the village to tell them what I had found and that it had made no difference and the ghosts would still appear?

As I pondered this, the growing light ahead of me illuminated another door. Like the entranceway where I had come in, it was a plain metal plate held within an archway. And, like the entranceway, the metal plate slid aside as I approached. Lights flickered into being on the other side, illuminating the chamber that lay beyond.

It was like nothing I had ever seen before, although it reminded me a little of the metal room where I had first encountered the man who claimed to be Odin. Was this, I wondered, a similar sky ship – no, I remembered, *space* ship – but one which had run aground here in Branscombe Wood?

Lights that had no flame flickered and pulsed on strange upright metal tables and metal boards. The air was suffused with a low hum and I could feel the faintest vibration in the floor beneath my feet as I stepped inside.

A figure rose up in front of me. In truth, I cannot say whether it appeared out of the air like the apparitions in the wood outside, or whether it simply stepped out from behind one of the panels. It was a woman. She was tall and slim with long fair hair. She wore a simple plain covering of silver and her deep, dark eyes held me in a steady gaze for a brief moment.

Then, in an instant, she was gone. Instead, I gazed back at the implacable visor of the knight of Agincourt. But I had seen enough to know it was not really him – even if I had not already surmised that he did not in reality exist at all. So, without fear, I took a step closer. And then another.

'What is this place?' I demanded.

The knight did not answer. Instead, he shimmered and blurred. When he again solidified before me, his aspect had changed and he was now the plague doctor.

'You should not be here,' he announced, voice echoing both inside his elongated mask and within the metal walls that surrounded us.

'I have every right to be here,' I countered. 'Indeed,' I went on, 'I think it is you who are misplaced. You have no right to be here, and nor does this great metal castle in which you live. If indeed you are alive in any real sense.'

'You are not like the other primitives,' the plague doctor said. Again, his outline shimmered and swam before me. This time it settled back into the fair-haired woman I had glimpsed when I first entered.

'Who are you?' I asked. 'I mean, who are you really?'

The woman looked at me with obvious amusement. 'The systems are reassessing you. There is no reason why we should not speak together while they complete their work. I am the Ship.'

This made no sense to me. How could a woman be a ship? But instead I asked: 'And is what I see now your true form?'

The woman laughed at that. 'I have no form, not as you understand it. I told you, I am the Ship. I am all around you. You called me a castle.'

'You are this whole building?' I asked, amazed and unsure quite what that could mean.

'In a sense. In another sense, I do not exist at all. I am certainly not alive in the way that you understand. What you see now, what is talking to you, is merely an avatar, a focal point, a construct for you to speak to and to speak to you.'

'And the ghosts outside?' I asked. 'Are they also constructed as you are?'

'In a way.' The woman, or whatever she really was, hesitated as if deciding if she should continue. 'I crash landed here,' she said after a few moments. 'Many, many years ago by your reckoning. I suffered a serious systems failure and made planetfall here. My crew was killed in the incident, so I am alone.'

I sensed a sadness in her at these words. I knew – and still know – what it is like to be alone. I waited to see if she would explain further, although I confess little of what she said made sense to me.

'The ghosts, as you call them, are a defence mechanism,' she went on at last. 'I must remain safe and undetected by the primitives. They would not understand. They might destroy me and harm themselves in the process. My systems reach into their minds, their memories, and pluck out images that seem strong and which will be respected or feared.'

'And these images become real?'

'They seem to. They are projected back into the primitives' minds to warn them away.'

'But you're frightening them,' I protested. 'There is a young woman in the village who you drove mad with your images.'

The woman's brow creased slightly in what might have been a puzzled frown. 'I cannot be held responsible for how primitive minds react to images that are taken from within those self-same minds. If their minds are so weak they can be damaged by their own memories, then that is not my fault.'

I was about to reply, about to tell her that I disagreed and that she should stop harming people and we could find another way to keep the villagers away from her strange metal castle. But I never got the chance. At that moment the lights around the room flashed furiously and a chatter of incoherent sound echoed round the chamber.

The woman stiffened. 'I understand,' she said.

'What was that?' I demanded.

'The assessment is complete,' the woman said calmly. 'Your presence, your words, your intelligence have all been evaluated. I am sorry.'

'Sorry?' I echoed. 'Sorry for what?'

Behind me, I heard the metal door slide shut. The woman began to blur again. Another figure formed out of her – one from my distant past. 'Father?' I gasped in surprise.

'I am sorry,' he said in the voice I remembered so dimly, so faintly from all those years ago. 'You have been assessed as a threat. You must be destroyed.'

With these words, he drew his great sword and stepped towards me. I stared in horror and astonishment. I knew he wasn't really my father. I knew he wasn't real at all. But I also had no doubt that he meant to kill me – either with the sword or by driving me out of my mind with more apparitions drawn from my memory.

There are so many memories I have struggled to forget, any one of which might drive me to distraction and leave me as broken and mindless as poor Jane. Any one of the pages torn from my journals so I would never have to read them again might do it.

Only when I felt the cold metal against my back did I realise that I had been moving away from the approaching figure. I ducked to one side as the sword cut through the air. I was under no illusions about how substantial this apparition was. It was no creature of the air like the others. The sword clanged off the metal plate, and I realised that this time the door had not opened as I neared it. I was trapped.

As my father who was not my father turned towards me, another figure appeared across the chamber. Again, it was a man from my past – my husband. He shook his head sadly, as if disappointed. Beside him, the knight from Agincourt was hefting his own sword while the plague doctor stepped from behind a panel.

There were more figures than I could count, fading into existence all around me. The king I had married, lepers I had watched die, friends long dead and enemies long forgotten. My husband Tomas, my lover Prince Karim. A dog-faced Caniform reared up, massive and brutal beside the Wizard of Marabia.

And my children, Essie, Johann and Rue, stared at me accusingly – as if asking how I could have let them die.

Out of panic as much as calculation, I ran for the nearest table of lights. These lights, I thought, must somehow be connected to the castle. Something here must control the doors and if only I could find it, I might open the door to the chamber and escape back into the woods.

There were things to press and others to turn. Small levers and tiny wheels, windows through which I could see thin strips of metal moving along a scale, text I could not read and all manner of things I could not begin to comprehend. Moving quickly to avoid swords and spears, trying desperately not to meet the gaze of any of the figures that followed me, I pressed and turned and twisted everything I could.

A sword slammed down into one of the tables, slicing deep into the metal where moments before my hand had been. A shower of sparks erupted from the metal wound. I twisted away, still pressing and turning and twisting whatever I could reach.

And then, suddenly, I was alone. The lighting deepened to a blood red. From somewhere deep within the castle came a sound – a mournful wail, building then falling. I knew instinctively that it must be an alarm of some sort, a warning.

'Ignition sequence activated,' a voice said. I turned sharply, but there was no one there. 'Ignition sequence activated,' the disembodied voice said again. 'Countdown begins.'

As I turned, looking for whoever was speaking, I saw that the door had opened. I ran towards it, but this time as I approached it started to close again. I hurled myself towards the shrinking gap between the door and its frame. The metal plate grazed my shoulder as it slammed shut. But, mercifully, I was through and back in the corridor. I ran, ignoring the pain in my shoulder.

The alarm was becoming louder and more insistent. The voice that came from everywhere and nowhere had started counting, but counting backwards. 'Twenty, nineteen…'

Finally, I saw the door where I entered this bizarre castle. But would it open? If it did not, there was nothing I could do about it.

'Fifteen,' the voice intoned. I had no idea what would happen when it ran out of numbers, but I was sure it wasn't good.

The voice reached ten as I approached the door. For an awful moment I thought it would stay closed, trapping me inside what would become my metal tomb. But then it slid open, and I sprinted out of the castle and towards the trees. Only when I heard a roar louder than any thunder did I turn and look back.

The castle, or ship, or whatever it was, burned. Fire erupted from beneath it and the whole immense structure seemed to lift slowly off the ground. But at once, it tilted to its side. The trees and vegetation growing through it held it back even as it struggled to rise into the sky. The fire beneath it burned brighter as the castle tilted still further. Then the whole structure was torn apart in a sudden brilliant ball of flame.

I hurled myself to the ground and covered my head. The heat washed over me, incredible and almost physical in its intensity as if I had been hit by a carriage. Then, it faded. When I dared to look, the castle was gone. Its remains burned brightly, a single oak tree standing defiantly in the midst of the inferno – the same tree as had been growing up and through the castle. Then its branches caught fire, and it too was engulfed in orange, yellow and red.

I walked slowly back to the village. Somehow I knew that, with the castle gone, there would be no more ghosts. The evening was setting in and dusk was falling by the time I made my way down into the valley.

Before I was halfway there, Edward and Maria and several others ran out to meet me. They demanded to know what had happened. Was I all right? Had I seen the fireball? They assumed it was a lightning strike that had caught one of the trees – but so big and fierce…

I told them little of what had happened. Only that they would have no more trouble with the ghosts of Branscombe Wood. Exhausted, I happily accepted Maria's soup and bread.

'You must stay with us,' Edward said. 'We owe you so much, the least we can do is accept you into our community. And,' he reminded me, 'you told us you have nowhere else to go.'

Had I told them that? It was true, and I was flattered by the offer. I told them I would sleep on it and let them know my answer in the morning.

But I knew it already. No matter how friendly and welcoming the villagers were, this was not the place I was looking for. I slept for several hours. Then, when the house was quiet and still, I crept downstairs and let myself out. I found my horse, grazing in a paddock behind the blacksmith's, and together we set off out of the village.

Not back towards the woods and the orange glow that lingered in the sky above them. But onwards in search of I knew not what. Just myself and my horse.

I patted him on the side of the neck as he carried me towards whatever awaited us. Perhaps, I thought, despite everything, I shall give him a name.

Also available from BBC Books:

BBC

DOCTOR WHO

Royal Blood

Una McCormack

ISBN 978 1 84990 992 1

The Grail is a story, a myth! It didn't exist on your world! It can't exist here!

The city-state of Varuz is failing. Duke Aurelian is the last of his line, his capital is crumbling, and the armies of his enemy, Duke Conrad, are poised beyond the mountains to invade. Aurelian is preparing to gamble everything on one last battle. So when a holy man, the Doctor, comes to Varuz from beyond the mountains, Aurelian asks for his blessing in the war.

But all is not what it seems in Varuz. The city-guard have lasers for swords, and the halls are lit by electric candlelight. Aurelian's beloved wife, Guena, and his most trusted knight, Bernhardt, seem to be plotting to overthrow their Duke, and Clara finds herself drawn into their intrigue...

Will the Doctor stop Aurelian from going to war? Will Clara's involvement in the plot against the Duke be discovered? Why is Conrad's ambassador so nervous? And who are the ancient and weary knights who arrive in Varuz claiming to be on a quest for the Holy Grail...?

An original novel featuring the Twelfth Doctor and Clara, as played by Peter Capaldi and Jenna Coleman

Also available from BBC Books:

BBC

DOCTOR WHO

Big Bang Generation

Gary Russell

ISBN 978 1 84990 991 4

I'm an archaeologist, but probably not the one you were expecting.

Christmas 2015, Sydney, New South Wales, Australia

Imagine everyone's surprise when a time portal opens up in Sydney Cove. Imagine their shock as a massive pyramid now sits beside the Harbour Bridge, inconveniently blocking Port Jackson and glowing with energy. Imagine their fear as Cyrrus 'the mobster' Globb, Professor Horace Jaanson and an alien assassin called Kik arrive to claim the glowing pyramid. Finally imagine everyone's dismay when they are followed by a bunch of con artists out to spring their greatest grift yet.

This gang consists of Legs (the sexy comedian), Dog Boy (providing protection and firepower), Shortie (handling logistics), Da Trowel (in charge of excavation and history) and their leader, Doc (busy making sure the universe isn't destroyed in an explosion that makes the Big Bang look like a damp squib).

And when someone accidentally reawakens the Ancients of Time – which, Doc reckons, wasn't the wisest or best-judged of actions – things get a whole lot more complicated...

An original novel featuring the Twelfth Doctor, as played by Peter Capaldi

Also available from BBC Books:

BBC

DOCTOR WHO

Deep Time

Trevor Baxendale

ISBN 978 1 84990 990 7

I do hope you're all ready to be terrified!

The Phaeron disappeared from the universe over a million years ago. They travelled among the stars using roads made from time and space, but left only relics behind. But what actually happened to the Phaeron? Some believe they were eradicated by a superior force… Others claim they destroyed themselves.

Or were they in fact the victims of an even more hideous fate?

In the far future, humans discover the location of the last Phaeron road – and the Doctor and Clara join the mission to see where the road leads. Each member of the research team knows exactly what they're looking for – but only the Doctor knows exactly what they'll find.

Because only the Doctor knows the true secret of the Phaeron: a monstrous secret so terrible and powerful that it must be buried in the deepest grave imaginable…

An original novel featuring the Twelfth Doctor and Clara, as played by Peter Capaldi and Jenna Coleman